THE ROCKING CHAIR BESIDE THE ROAD

A Novel

BY

DR. JIMMY F. SELLARS

To: Ron + Mitsy,
Jimmy Sellars
Hope you enjoy
for Mattie and
Uncle Lee

Other books by this author:

Do You Know Sammy? (A Bullied Child)

A New Preacher For Turnbow, Arkansas

An Email From Mandy

Mandy's Story

Mandy's Family Returns To Dodd Mtn.

ISBN: 1499316917

ISBN 13: 9781499316919

Library of Congress Control Number: 2014908205

CreateSpace Independent Publishing Platform

North Charleston, South Carolina

TABLE OF CONTENTS

CHAPTER ONE

THIS IS ELBOW, ARKANSAS

"Joe, when we make the turn up ahead, I want you to look at some of the unusual things in this community," Jake said as he drove his bread truck along the road.

The next community Jake referred to was called Elbow. The name was appropriate because the highway made a ninety degree turn in the middle of what at one time was a small town. By 1969 all that remained of the town was two stores that were no longer open to the public, what at one time would have been a large three-story building that certainly looked out of place in this area, a cemetery by a rather large church, several smaller buildings that could have been stores or offices, and several older houses and buildings.

"What kind of unusual things am I suppose to be looking for Jake?" Joe asked. "It seems to me everything I have seen on this route has been unusual."

"I know Joe, you being from New York, everything seems strange to you in this up-class area of Arkansas. I know it will take time for you to adjust to our advanced ways here, but just take it easy and watch me so that I can teach you how to relate to all these nice folks on our route," Jake suggested.

Joe had moved to the Ozarks from upper-state New York after a serious automobile accident, that his mother-in-law blamed on his drinking. The accident had taken the lives of his wife and two children. With his mother-in-law blaming him for their deaths, he had decided to give up a rather successful business, fine home, and several friends and move to an area that was advertised as a place where people minded their own business and left outsiders alone. That was what Joe needed at the present, but how he had been talked into taking this job driving a bread truck was beyond his understanding.

He had met Jake at the local coffee shop in Turnbow and by some strange way of talking to him in a language called English that he didn't really understand, he found himself telling Jake that he would help run the route during the summer.

From the first day that Joe had arrived in town, it was clear to him that people had a nosy interest in outsiders. Even his effort at walking down the few streets of the town brought looks from everyone he met that told him of their concern about him being there. Any effort to communicate brought a quick double look and response that let him know that he wasn't from that area. But Joe had decided to make the best of the situation. Surely after a few months he would be accepted, and he could adjust to living in a quiet rural area and begin the process of putting his life back together.

At least he thought he might get his life back together if he could learn how to avoid a Rev. Martin that seemed to be on every street corner in the small town and always greeted him with a rather strange look. It was a look that gave Joe the feeling that Rev. Martin knew things about his past that he had never told and didn't intend to tell.

And then there was Mrs. Dobbins at the grocery store. Every visit to the store gave Mrs. Dobbins an opportunity to prove that she had declared herself to be the match maker to provide Joe with the perfect match. Joe always attempted to be the New England gentleman that Mrs. Dobbins expected him to be and listen with great interest to every word she had to say about different single women in the area.

Joe couldn't leave Gracie Barns out of his list of nosy people in town. Joe's mind just could not forget what every trip to the post office was like. Gracie Barns ran the small post office in town and made it her business to pry into the content of any mail Joe received. Gracie made it known to Joe on every visit that she might be a little older than some of the men in town but was available to the right man, "any" man would have been more correct. It was Joe's opinion that Gracie had been turned down by more men than any woman he knew. He tried to make it clear, in his New England gentlemen's way that he wasn't interested and was rejecting her also.

Jake's sudden stop to avoid an older man in a truck brought Joe back to the present situation and Jake's last statement. He struggled for a moment to think through what Jake had said. It was something about everything in the Ozarks being more advanced than in New England. Yes, that was it. Jake thought it would be difficult for Joe to fit in to the more modern ways of the Ozarks.

"I don't know about all the "advanced" ways you are talking about. We have already made six stops on this route, and every-thing I have seen and heard seems several years behind what I grew up with in New York," Joe responded. "Now, what am I to be looking for in this community you called Elbow?"

"There are several things about this com-munity that I find interesting," Jake said. "As we enter the town you will notice a cem-etery with the most ununsual tombstone right at the front by the gate. In the town you will see two old stores that have been closed for years, but they have not been torn down. In the middle of town, there is a building that looks completely out of place for a small town in Arkansas, and at the edge of town you will see a trophy case beside the road with trophies in it. Just outside of town after we make the ninety degree turn, you will see large oak trees with an old man sitting in a rocking chair. I tell you it is all very interesting."

"Only in the Ozarks would I expect to hear something like this. You mean to tell me that you find all these things you have just listed as strange?" Joe asked.

"Oh, hell, I should have guessed. You are going to tell me that these kinds of things exist in every community in New York. I should have just asked you to explain them to me and not made a big deal over the fact that they are here in Elbow," Jake said with an irritated tone in his voice.

"Wait a minute. You should have asked me to explain them. You mean you don't know what they mean? How long have you been driving this route through this area?" Joe asked with a surprised look on his face.

"This is my tenth year, but I am not the type to pry into other folks business," Jake answered.

"Oh, no I can tell you aren't the type. You just drive through this area two times a week for ten years and wonder about things, but you don't stop and ask. Now that makes good Ozark sense to me," Joe responded as he broke into a rather strange laugh that made Jake feel as though he might be making fun of him.

"See that, now tell me you have grave markers like that in New York," Jake interrupted Joe's laugh to point out the rather large tombstone by the gate of the cemetery.

"Well, I will say that is about the strangest marker I have seen. However, there are several in New York that are as large or even larger but not made quite like that one," Joe admitted.

As they moved on through what had been the town of Elbow, Jake pointed out the old store buildings. He was sure there was some kind of interesting story behind those buildings. Next he slowed at the large building with strange windows and hallways, and last the trophy case that suggested that at one time the town had a very successful ball team of some kind.

When they appoached the Oak trees, Jake had slowed to a very slow speed. The rocking chair was under the trees, and the old fellow that Jake had mentioned was sitting in the rocker.

"There he is, just as I told you he would be. It never fails if it isn't raining, he will be sitting in that rocker," Jake explained.

"Why don't you just stop and talk to him? He might be able to tell you about the town and all those things you find so interesting about Elbow," Joe asked.

"You'll have to learn that folks in the Ozarks aren't like the people from the New England area. We don't pry into people's lives around here, besides by this time next year, it won't matter," Jake answered.

"What do you mean it won't matter?" Joe asked.

"The rumor is that one of those honest elected officials that we sent to the big house to take care of us has taken care of himself by purchasing the land north of here. He plans on having the highway bypass Elbow across his land so that he can build a gas stop, cafe, and other buildings designed to take your money. By next year you will be travelling on his new road, and Elbow will no longer exist," Jake explained.

CHAPTER TWO

MEET UNCLE LEE

The summer passed quickly for Joe. The routes had turned into a rather routine process. Mondays and Thursdays the route covered mostly rural stores that were located in communities like Cane Valley, Hickory Ridge, Mortonville, Grapevine, Dodd Mountain, Timberline, Turnbow, Nogo, Center Point, and Snowball. The Tuesday and Friday route was around three of the larger towns and required more work. Wednesday Joe helped Jake in the bakery. This provided a change of pace that Joe appreciated.

The Monday and Thursday route did take Joe through Elbow. This always gave

Joe the opportunity to ask Jake if he wanted to stop and visit the elderly fellow in the rocking chair that set beside the road in Elbow. Since there were eighteen small stores on this route, Jake always used time as an excuse not to stop.

All these eighteen stores shared most things in common. They were all family owned. This meant that either the husband or wife was in the store at the time deliveries were made. The buildings were older buildings that were too small for the number of items the owners tried to stock. This always provided limited shelf space for the bread and bakery products that Jake wanted to leave in the store.

Jake's routine was to check to see how many items had been sold and how many needed to be replaced because of age. He would return to the truck and place the new items in a box and return to the store to stock the shelf, write up a ticket, have the owner sign it, receive his money, and make a statement or two about the weather or community and move on to the next store. It was a routine that Joe found to be anything but fulfilling, but he was only working for the summer and it was already August.

The last Friday in August, changed Joe's thinking about what the future might hold. Jake called in sick and Joe was left to run the Friday route by himself. When Joe returned to the bread factory at the end of the day he was called to the office. Here he was informed that Jake had been taken to the hospital with kidney stones and would not be available for work the following week.

Since it was late August the owner, Mr. Gulley, did not intend to hire anyone for just a week. This meant that Joe would have all the work by himself the following week. It was a responsibility Joe was sure he was capable of handling but one he wasn't sure he wanted.

Over the weekend Joe ran the stops over in his mind and the process Jake used at each stop in dealing with the store owners. It was during that time that Joe thought of Elbow. If the route was to be his responsibility then he would rush through the stops on Monday and gain enough time to stop in Elbow and visit with this elderly man in the rocking chair.

Monday was a clear, warm day and Joe was sure the rocking chair would be beside the road, so he made his stops as quickly as possible. He had to explain at every stop why Jake was not with him and that it was only for the one week. He assured the store owners that Jake would be back.

As Joe made the elbow turn he could see the chair under the Oak trees. It was at this point that he became a little uneasy. Thinking about stopping and talking to this stranger had not been a problem for him. He had dealt with a lot of people in many different situations in New England, but all of a sudden this seemed different. All the warning Jake had given him about being nosy and asking people in this area questions about their personal lives ran through his mind like a bullet.

There must have been a reason why this fellow was always by himself. Maybe he didn't want people to visit with him. Maybe he had made that clear to the people in the area in the past and they had learned to leave him alone. Now Joe thought that maybe he should have followed Jake's advice and left him alone too.

As Joe approached the trees it was as if he wasn't in control of the bread truck and without any effort to take control, the truck came to a stop. As he looked to the trees two eyes as cold as steel were staring at him from the rocker. Joe was looking at a rather large man dressed in older overalls with a plaid shirt. He had to be in his late eighties or even nineties. He had lost most of his grey hair, and it appeared as though he had not shaved for a day or two. Joe slowly opened the door to the truck and stood beside the truck. He had wanted to make this stop all summer and now that he had, he couldn't think of a thing to say.

"Got some kind of trouble with your truck?" an uninviting voice asked from the rocker.

"No, sir, just been helping Jake Crooker with this route all summer and been wanting to stop and see if you could tell me anything about the area," Joe responded without thinking.

"Don't believe I have heard anyone talk like that from around here before. You must be from up North," the elderly man replied.

"Yes, sir, I am from New York. I moved to Turnbow less than a year ago," Joe answered.

"Bet that has caused the folks from Turnbow to ask you a lot of questions. Why are you interested in this area? You part of the elected folks who plan on building the new road around Elbow?" the man asked.

"No, sir, I don't know anything about elected people or new roads. I am just interested in some of the buildings in the town," Joe said.

"Thinking you might want to buy one or two and fix them up are you?" the man asked.

"No, I don't really have the money to do anything like that. I am just interested in the history of places like Elbow, and I thought you might be able to share some of that history with me," Joe replied.

"Well, I guess I have been in this area longer than anyone else so that ought to mean that I could tell you more about it's history than anyone else. At least I can tell it the way I want it told," the old fellow said with a chuckle.

"You lived here all your life?" Joe asked.

"No, lived in Flint Rock in Fulton County first two years. I have been here about ninety-four I guess," was his answer.

"That would make you about ninety-six years old. You have seen a lot of the history of this town," Joe said with a surprised look on his face. He could not believe that a person would live that long in one place. "You say you were born in Fulton County."

"Sure was, I think about 1873 or so. You don't try to keep up with stuff like that after a while. Family moved there in a covered wagon from Tennessee after the big war. Folks lived in the wagon while Pa built a cabin. I was born in the wagon before the cabin was finished," the elderly man began.

"There wouldn't be much room in a wagon would there?" Joe asked.

"Not much, according to the way Ma used to tell the story, Pa and my two brothers slept on the ground under the wagon and Ma and my sister slept in the wagon. Pa fixed a crate for me to sleep in so that no one would step on me. Not much room, but I guess they made out. After two years in Flint Rock, my sister died of the fever and we moved here. Pa built a cabin on that ridge over yonder and when I reached twenty years of age I met this pretty young girl. I built this house, married and raised my family. I've lived here all the rest of the time," he explained.

The house that the elderly man referred to certainly looked seventy years old to Joe. It was a small house with about three rooms and in bad need of repair. Joe was sure that if the house had ever had any paint, it was many years ago and had long since disappeared. The tin roof was covered with a layer of reddish-brown rust that suggested the possibility of a leak or two in a heavy rain. The porch that ran the length of the house had several boards that appeared to be rotten and some even appeared to be missing from around the front of the house. There wasn't an electric line running to the house which let Joe know that the house didn't have any modern appliances, not even lighting.

From the way the owner was dressed, Joe was convinced that none of this really mattered to him. He seemed at peace with himself and the world. This was a setting that made Joe wonder if it was the positions that people worked for that brought happiness, or a life style that provided the happiness. This old fellow certainly seemed content in his setting, and it was clear that he had very few positions. Joe's mind went back to his childhood and some of the verses from the Bible that his teacher had taught him about peace of mind and happiness. For this old man he was convinced that it was a state of the mind that provided him all the happiness he needed to have a satisfying life.

"I don't think I have introduced myself," Joe said. "I am Joe Harrison."

"Well, Joe Harrison, all the folks around here call me Uncle Lee. I guess you can do the same. I ain't related to any of the folks that call me uncle but they seem to like that name. Had a wife and five children but they are all gone. Wife died in child birth with the sixth child in 1911, I reckon," Uncle Lee continued. "Pa died five or six years after I got married. He had been wounded in the war. He fought for the South. Fought from Tennessee to Georgia and around but never did talk about it. He always said that you did things in a war you didn't want to tell your family. Ma lived several years after that, but they are all gone now. It is just me now. It has been that way for some twenty years I reckon."

"And you say you have lived here all of your life. Have you never been out of this county?" Joe asked.

"I went to Little Rock one time when I was about twenty-two or three I reckon. I had just been married about two years when some of the farmers here decided to drive their cattle, hogs, and goats to Little Rock to sell them. You couldn't get anything for animals around here at that time. My dad had several cows and some hogs he wanted to send so I went along," Uncle Lee explained.

It was seventy-five miles from Crossroads to Little Rock. At that time there were only dirt roads and no bridges. The people from the area put their animals together and men drove them to the market just north of the river in the Little Rock area.

"We have four wagons going along this year to carry food for the animals and supplies for us. Three of the wagons have chickens and geese," Milford Williams told the men.

"I think we can make about ten to fifteen miles a day depending on the animals and weather," Veron said. "If prices are good this year we should do alright."

"I sure hope these young men who have never seen the big city don't cause us a lot of trouble. Sometimes seeing all the things the big city has to offer is more than they can take," Milford told the older men.

"We might just leave them with the animals outside of town and enjoy the city life for a day or two ourselves," Veron suggested.

"I guess I had forgotten that you were the one who caused us all the trouble three years ago when we made the drive. Maybe we will need to leave you with the animals," Harry responded.

"If you hadn't tried to impress that woman in the sleeping house I would not have gotten into trouble. I was just trying to save you from her sisters," Veron explained.

The drive required that the men keep all the animals together and moving along the trails that served as roads in the mid-1890's. There were many creeks that had to be crossed along the way. Sometimes it was difficult to get the animals to cross and valuable time was lost.

At night the men slept under the wagons. They would take turns watching the animals and sleeping. At daybreak the good cooks in the group would prepare a fast meal and the group would be on their way.

By the fifth day the group from Crossroads began to meet up with others on their way to Little Rock. This was a sign to the ones who had made the trip in the past that they were getting close to the big city. On day seven they had their animals at the holding pens and people interested in buying what they had for sale were making offers.

Milford acted as the agent for the group. Once he had the price he thought was fair he sold everyone's animals. After the sale everyone made their way over the only river bridge they saw on the trip into the city of Little Rock.

Milford gave the three young men a dollar each and told them to stay out of trouble. He attempted to explain what trouble would look like, but the young men were sure they could take care of themselves.

Lee, Joe, and Claude spent the day looking at things they had never seen before. They had seen drunk men before, but by night some of the drunks did things that were not common in Crossroads. Fights were common at the sleeping house over the night and none of the men got that much rest. By morning they were all ready to return to the quiet life that Crossroads had to offer.

"I reckon I never did have any desire to see the big city again after that,' Uncle Lee told Joe. "Everything I ever wanted was right here so there wasn't any need to go off looking for anything."

"I sure would like to stay longer and visit with you, but I have got to get back on my bread route. Maybe I can stop by again and we can talk about the history of Elbow," Joe suggested as he rushed back toward his truck.

"Stop by any time," Uncle Lee offered.

As Joe drove toward his next stop, he rolled over everything he had learned from the elderly man in the rocking chair beside the road. Here was the last of his kind in this area. If only he had written a book of these interesting events that had taken place, Joe thought. Joe realized that summer was about over and Jake would be returning to run the route. He knew that he had enjoyed his first and probably only meeting with a very interesting man, Uncle Lee.

———— CHAPTER THREE ————

THE TOWN FEUD

Jake returned to work on Monday as promised, but the pain he experienced from kidney stones told Joe that he might be running the bread route by himself again in the near future. This possibility didn't bother Joe as much now that he had met Uncle Lee of Elbow and discovered what an interesting person he was. His ability to remember events from the past created a desire in Joe's mind to stop and gain more information about this strange place.

By Wednesday Jake had taken all of the pain he could stand and informed Joe that the rest of the week would be his. Joe had looked at the old fellow in the rocking chair on Monday and witnessed a slight wave from him as the bread truck passed. He was eager to run the route on Thursday and stop by to talk with Uncle Lee. The weather was pretty and warm for the time of year, and he was sure he would be in the chair waiting for him to pass.

Thursday morning Joe reported to work early. He knew that he would not be able to start the route any earlier than usual because the first stores on the route didn't open until six o'clock, but he wanted to make sure everything was ready to go. He planned on being at the first stop as soon as the owner opened. He would rush through the rest of the stops so that he could have as much time with Uncle Lee as possible.

It was a warm day and the rocking chair was in place under the Oak trees just as Joe had hoped. He had created several questions in his mind that he wanted to ask but wasn't sure how far he should go without seeming nosy. As he pulled the bread truck to a stop by the trees, he decided to let the conversation develop along the lines of whatever Uncle Lee wanted to talk about.

"Kinda thought you might stop Monday, but saw the other driver with you. I guess you had a busy day," Uncle Lee greeted Joe.

"No, sir, it wasn't that busy but Jake is always in a hurry. He is having problems with kidney stones again this week. I drive for him when he is out," Joe responded.

"Yeah, I have watched him drive by for years. I always seemed to think he wanted to stop but was afraid to for some reason. Seems like younger folks don't want to talk to old people. Guess they think we don't know anything to tell or something," Uncle Lee added.

"Last time I stopped you told me how long you had lived here in Elbow. I would like to know what happened to the town. At one time it must have been a rather large town for this area," Joe said as he attempted to get the conversation turned to the history of the area.

"Yeah, one time it was. Wasn't always called Elbow you know. Guess the outsiders changed the name about '54 or 5. Til then it was known as Crossroads. The town feud in '49 closed the roads running east and south and left the elbow in town. When the state paved the road in '54 the elbow was created and the town got a new name," Uncle Lee explained.

"In the 40's the town had three doctors, several stores, a large school with a band and ball teams, four churches, the big hotel you see in town, and several homes. It was a busy place, and people came here from all over to shop," Uncle Lee continued. "Guess the ball team winning the state tournament in '42 started the downfall, but it was the feud of '49 that really changed things around here."

"What kind of town feud are we talking about? Did some of the town's people get in a fight?" Joe asked.

"More of a war of words than anything I reckon. It developed over a complete misunderstanding, but no one could do anything to get it straightened out. Dr. Gus Rodgers had a little dentist shop up the east end of town. Sadie Walker went by one Monday morning to have two upper teeth pulled. Now Sadie was built like these modern day football players, but she tried to give everyone the impression that she was the prettiest of the movie stars. She had a way of suggesting to men that she was really interested in them, but refused any of their offers. Too good for anyone in the town was the way she acted I reckon. She grew up on the poorest farm in the county, but she tried to pretend that she came from New York or some place like that. Well, old Gus at a hundred twenty-five pounds and seventy years of age was having some real problems pulling her teeth, so he placed his knee in her lap and put his left hand on her chest. That's what started it all I reckon," Uncle Lee said as he paused to get his breath.

"I think I see what might have happened next, but how did that situation develop into a town feud?" Joe asked with a puzzled look on his face.

"Sadie quickly responded to her misunderstanding of Old Gus's intentions and ran over him as she tried to get out of his office. It just happened that Pete Albright was taking a load of saw logs down the street on his big wagon with a four hitch. When Sadie ran into the street to alarm everyone that she was being molested by Old Gus, Pete's four hitch broke to run and pulled the wagon load of logs into the 'only ones' church," Uncle Lee explained.

"I don't guess I know that kind of church," Joe interrupted. "It must be a local movement that we did not have in New York."

"Reckon it had another name, but we always called them the 'only ones' because they were always preaching that they would be the only ones in heaven, or something. Anyway, the church had a big meeting going, so they had left the stoves full of wood for the Monday night meeting. When the logs from Pete's wagon hit the little wood framed building, the stoves were knocked off their stands and a fire broke out in the church.

Pete's mules broke free of the wagon and pulling the tongue and front wheels of the wagon, they headed south down what was main street at that time. The tongue and wheels waved back and forth taking out about everything on buildings they hit.

There were other wagons and four or five trucks along the street. The mules and horses hooked to the wagons began to run, and before you knew it, the street was full of wagon parts, porches from the stores, picket fences and other things.

With the wind out of the north, it wasn't long until several buildings were on fire and with all that the mules had done to the buildings, it was difficult for the men to form any kind of way of stopping the flames. By the time the fire settled on Tuesday morning, most of the buildings to the south of town were gone," Uncle Lee stopped for another breath and to see how Joe was taking in his story.

"You would have thought that all these friendly Ozark folks would have joined together to help rebuild those buildings. I don't see how such a tragic turn of events would have caused a feud. I must be missing something in your story," Joe responded.

With that response Uncle Lee settled back in his rocker and closed his eyes. He began to tell the rest of the story in such clear detail that Joe began to think that he was back on the streets of Elbow (Crossroads) in 1949 and witnessing every event as it took place. He could just hear the people talking and see them interacting with each other as Uncle Lee told his story.

The folks from town and surrounding areas who had come to witness the fire stood on the street Tuesday morning looking at the smoltering rubble. Most were exhausted from their effort at stopping the fire, and several were rather short tempered.

"I guess Pete will have the devil to pay when all is said and done about this," Josh Calhoun said as he winked at Sam Newman.

"The devil to pay I would say. The devil to pay, you don't even know who to give credit to for this act that has come to your town. I have been sharing the truth of the Gospel in this town for a week," the Gospel speaker from the church on the corner interrupted in a loud voice. "I have been preaching that God was going to deliver fire upon this sinful town if you didn't repent and you would not listen. Now you can see what He has done and you deserve every bit of it. I tell you fall on your knees here and now or even geater things than this will come to this town."

"Sir, I think you are out of place with your statements," the pastor from the church across the street on the north side of town shouted. "We don't know your God of anger and destruction. The God we worship is a loving God. He would not do anything like this to our town. The folks in this town are good people. I think you need to ask their forgiveness in what you have accused them of being."

"I will repeat what I said," the Gospel speaker attempted to say as folks from the town, exhausted from fighting the fire, began to leave the area. "Repent I tell you, repent now before it is too late for this town!"

"Pete, I would say you have done just about as much to kill this town as closing the school did," Josh Calhoun said to Pete as he walked by him on the way back to his store.

"Well, Josh I guess this would be a good time for me to tell you what you have done to kill this town! You and your high prices in your store. You are just sore because I never did shop with you. Hell, I ain't going to be taken for my hard earned money just to suit you," Pete responded in a very angry tone of voice that caused Josh's face to turn red from anger.

"You may not have spent your hard earned money in my store, but before these folks are through with you, they will take all you have," Josh said shouting at the top of his voice.

When Rev. Franklin from the church on the upper side of town heard the two men, he ran to separate them before they started throwing punches. He made his way between the two just in time to hear Sadie Walker telling her story to Maud Goodman. It was clear from what Sadie said that she was blaming Dr. Rodgers for everything that had happened.

"Now Sadie, you should not spread rumors about this event. We have just lost a church, three stores, a doctor's office, and four houses. This is a difficult time for Crossroads," Rev. Franklin told Sadie.

"Well! Listen to that, a man of the cloth standing up for his best paying member. What else would you expect from the leader of a church with members who think they are better than the rest of us folks," Sadie responded in a voice so loud that all the people in the area turned to see what was happening. "For your information Rev. Franklin, I guess I have the facts, and I have them first hand. I tell you Dr. Rodgers was trying to molest me. Everyone knows that Clara has been turning a cold shoulder to him ever since she learned that he doesn't have any money. He gave it all to your church, I have heard."

Clara was Dr. Rodgers' second wife. His first wife had passed away in childbirth some forty years earlier. Dr. Rodgers had not remarried until he met Clara Blake ten years ago. Clara was twenty years younger than Dr. Rodgers, but when this pretty, aggressive woman made a move to catch him, he did not refuse.

Folks in the area all thought that Clara had married Dr. Rodgers for his money, but he didn't care about that because he knew if that was her reason, the last laugh would be on her. He had given just about everything he had made over the years to the church, but he led the town folks to believe that he was rather well off. The deception had worked until out of anger over his younger sister calling him a doddering old fool, he let the cat out of the bag. It just happened that Clara was in the kitchen and overheard what he said. Their relationship had been as Sadie suggested since that day.

From one end of town to the other, arguments broke out among the local folks about who was to blame. It was clear from the way the blame was being passed around that many of the folks had hard feelings against others in town that had been hidden for years. The fire was just an opportunity for them to air those feelings even though they had nothing to do with the reason for the fire.

After some time of arguing, exhausted from fighting the fire, people began to make their way to their stores and homes. Some offered those who had lost homes a place to stay, but in general, people went their separate ways.

"Josh, it looks like it only took you two days to change the prices on just about everything in your store since the fire took out two of your competitors. I didn't think I would ever see the folks in Crossroads become so greedy," Dr. Gant said as he walked through the store looking at the items Josh had for sale.

"I don't know how you would know what my prices were since you always did your shopping at Samuel's General Store on the south end of town," Josh quickly responded. "A man has got to make a living you know. Besides, you are not one to complain about prices; you have always been higher on your services than Dr. Hickey."

"Don't know how you would know about my prices; I don't think any of your family has ever used any of my services. You are right about one thing, a man does have to make a fair living. Taking advantage of folks in times like these is another matter, I think. If all the folks leave this area who are talking about leaving, you may be giving some of these items away," Dr. Gant said as he turned to leave the store.

"I haven't heard of any folks leaving Crossroads. What are you talking about?" Josh asked.

"Ella and I have decided to move to Snowball. We had been talking about it since they closed the school and our children have to travel so far to Center Point. I guess Jack and Sarah Sharp will be leaving. Most of their income came from boarding students who came here to our high school. They lost that income with the closing of the school and now the fire has taken everything they owned. Tom and Hanna Wiggins also boarded students, and they plan on moving since they lost their house in the fire. Harry Martin told me that he was closing his blacksmith shop because people were buying trucks and no longer needed his service. I think he said he was moving to Hickory. I think others will follow. There isn't much left here to hold folks anymore," Dr. Gant answered.

"Uncle Lee, I have lost track of time!" Joe said as he looked at his watch.

"I must be going. Maybe I will be able to stop again in the future. But you must tell me what happened to the street on the east side of town. It wasn't involved in the fire," Joe said as he stood to his feet to leave.

"Well, the folks who had been burned out couldn't afford to rebuild, so they closed that part of town. The blame was so rough on Dr. Rodgers that Clara decided to close his office and move him to Turnbow. Harry's blacksmith shop was being replaced by a shop on the west end of town that worked on cars and trucks. The school that was the main reason for the street, had been closed because of the boys winning the state basketball championship. There wasn't any need for a street running east anymore," Uncle Lee explained.

"I sure would like to know how a team winning a championship could close a school, but I have got to be on my way. Maybe that can be a story for another day," Joe said as he returned to the bread truck and waved goodbye to Uncle Lee.

CHAPTER FOUR

THE TROPHY CASE

When Joe returned to the factory with his bread truck on Friday afternoon he had a message telling him that he was to meet with Mr. Gulley, the owner of the bread company, in his office. Joe knew what the note meant but wasn't disappointed. He had already worked for three weeks longer than his summer employment had required. The work had not been difficult, but the one twenty-five per hour he had received in pay was certainly much less than he had made in New York. It had provided eating money and Joe was content with that.

Joe had never really figured out why Mr. Gulley had agreed to Jake's request for an additional hand for the summer. The routes Jake ran didn't require that much work, but with Jake's kidney stones the knowledge of the routes had made it easy for Joe to fill in for several runs.

Mr. Gulley was a rather large man with a pleasant personality. It was clear from his size that he enjoyed a lot of the things that they produced in the factory. The fact that he often had something to eat in his hands proved that. He was always working alongside the other employees in the factory or helping repair something that had broken down. Joe had found him to be an honest person who was really interested in his employees and their well-being.

Joe thought over the advantages of being free from the employment as he walked to Mr. Gulley's office. He would now be able to complete some of the work he had begun in the spring on the small house he had purchased near Turnbow. He would also be able to continue the work he had begun on a book he was writing. It had always been a desire of his to write novels, and moving to the Ozarks and meeting Uncle Lee had given him a lot of ideas about things he could put in books. There were plenty of interesting people and stories in this area of the country that Joe thought needed to be shared in written form.

The outer office where two young women did all the paper work was neat and well arranged. One thing that Mr. Gulley was known for was hiring people who were well qualified for their jobs. When Joe entered Mr. Gulley's office it was easy to see why he needed qualified help. His office was everything but well arranged and neat.

Behind boxes stacked to the ceiling was a desk with forms and paper work stacked so high that you could barely see Mr. Gulley. After comments about what he intended to do someday, Mr. Gulley explained to Joe that Jake would be returning on Monday so his services would no longer be needed. Mr. Gulley thanked Joe for his summer work and gave him the normal line of if he ever needed a job to check with him.

With goodbyes said, Joe was on his way back home to his small house just outside Turnbow. On Sunday an unusual weather front from the north blew through the area. The front brought with it a rather large amount of cold rain that lasted through Tuesday. Joe was sure that the sudden change in the weather meant that Uncle Lee would no longer be sitting in his rocker. He wondered if it would be possible to visit with him in his home. The only way Joe knew to answer that question was to drive over to Elbow and see. This he decided to do on Friday.

Joe awoke to a second cold front on Friday morning. The wind was blowing from the north and the rain was very cold, but he had made the decision to travel to Elbow and the weather would not stop him. He wanted to stop by the trophy case first and then he would travel on to Uncle Lee's house.

Inside the trophy case was evidence that Crossroads High School had been a school with several outstanding senior boys' basketball teams. There were several trophies with county champs on them, a number of invitational tournament names on them, four had district champs, a state runner-up trophy from '40, and one had state champs in '42. There had to be a story here and Joe wanted Uncle Lee to tell it as only he could.

When Joe drove into Uncle Lee's yard and walked toward the porch, he could hear someone pulling a bow across the strings of a fiddle. While Joe didn't know that much about music, he could tell that at one time this player was good. It was clear to Joe that only time had taken its toll on the fingers of this player, and he could no longer make the sounds on the fiddle he once could. This had to be Uncle Lee.

Joe knocked on the door and was greeted with Uncle Lee's response, 'it's open.' Joe made his way into the two- room house. It was dark inside since there were no electric lights. An old bed was in the lefthand corner of what was a living room. A wood stove set in the middle of the room and a large, old organ sat to the left of the door. Uncle Lee was sitting in a rocker similar to the one under the Oak trees, and a second chair was near the wood stove. One picture was hanging on the wall. It looked like it might be a picture of the governor of the state. Joe couldn't tell for sure.

"I see you can play the fiddle," Joe began.

"Use to, can't play much any more. Fingers drawn so I can't get them to do what they are suppose to," Uncle Lee explained.

"You play the organ too?" Joe asked.

"Did years ago, also played the trumpet. We had a band that played at the ball games and special events around here abouts," Uncle Lee answered.

"I stopped on the way over and looked at the trophy case. Looks like Crossroads was known for its basketball teams. You said a few weeks ago that it was the ball team's winning the state tournament that caused the town to lose its school. Can you tell me how that happened?" Joe asked.

"All started about '38 I reckon. Crossroads hired two of the best men for coaches in the state. They were local fellows who had played ball here a few years back. By '40 the coaches had the boys ready for a run at the state tournament. They would have won it had it not been for the fever. All the boys got sick the week of the tournament and by Saturday night and the finals they were too sick to take the win," Uncle Lee explained.

"I still don't see how a school developing a championship basketball team could cost the community it's school," Joe responded. "There has to be more to this story than just boys playing basketball."

"Guess you being from the East you don't understand how important the basketball team was to a community around here in the '40's," Uncle Lee replied. "The basketball season was the center of life for a town back then. Folks came from everywhere to watch the good teams play. They spent money in town and at the school. It kept the community going during hard times. The towns with smaller schools were being forced to close their schools, and the students were required to travel miles to larger schools. If you had a good ball team parents wanted their children to come to your school."

Joe listened with a great deal of interest and concern that this story was being told to Uncle Lee's way of understanding. He had heard of school consolidation in the south and many other areas. It had even taken place in his home town, but it wasn't based on the ball team's but the school's ability to provide and maintain what was considered quality education for the students. However, Joe decided not to interrupt Uncle Lee's version of the story and see where it was going.

"Crossroads had beaten Center Point in the district the year before, that would have been '41 I reckon. Because of that loss some talk suggested that Center Point School might be moved to Crossroads. Folks at Center Point were so jealous that they vowed they would never lose to Crossroads again. Well, by early in the season, it was clear that the '42 team was even better than the '41 team. When Center Point heard how good the Crossroads team was, they bought out the committee to get the district tournament at their place. Stories were told all winter about how they planned on paying the officials to throw the game to them so that they could go to the state tournament," Uncle Lee told the event as if he were sure he was correct in everything he was saying.

At that point Uncle Lee began to relive that season with a tone of voice and expression on his face that seemed to suggest that he took great pleasure in being a part of the fan club of '42. It was clear to Joe that the season of '42 had changed Crossroads alright, and he was sure that somewhere in Uncle Lee's story the truth of why it changed was found.

"Good morning Coach," Sam Cato said to Coach Max Lester as he walked into the store. "Boys sure looked good last night against Nogo. I think you and Dick have them ready for a good season and another run at the state."

"Sam, that was the first game. It is going to be a long season and anything can happen, but they sure did look good for the first game," Coach Lester answered with a tone of satisfaction about how the team had played.

"And who would ever have thought of having the community band play at a ball game?" Maggie Wilson joined in. "It sure got the fans involved, even though I don't think it would have taken anything else to set them off. They may have played just a little too loud at times, but I am sure you will address that when you meet with them."

"Well, Maggie I don't think I have ever seen you at a game before. Can't say I saw you there last night with such a full gym, but I will see what I can do about the community band," Coach Lester replied.

"It's Miss Maggie, Max Lester and you might want to see what you can do about the way Bobby Joe wrote the scores up on the board. At times you couldn't tell what his numbers were. It was clear that he hasn't improved some things since I had him in the third grade," Maggie added as she walked by the coach to the door.

"Guess Maggie may not be your best fan Coach," Will Gifford said as he reached out to shake hands with Coach Lester. "Seems like I can remember you having problems with your numbers when she was our third grade teacher."

"I think we will have a good crowd over at Hickory Friday night. We don't intend to let the locals over there beat us this year with their homemade rules and callers," Arthur Hale added as everyone in the store joined in the conversation.

By the end of the regular season it was clear that Crossroads had a good ball team. They had played every school in the county along with Thirty-Six, Lead Hill, and Flat Plains and had not lost a game.

Communities did not take kindly to the visiting team winning on their floors and fights were common among the fans. Losing teams always complained of unsportsman like play from the winning players, but over-all it had been a good season.

"Have you seen the schedule for the district tournament?" Tyler Nelson asked the fellows at the barber shop. "They have placed Ash Grove and Wild Cherry on our side of the schedule. We will have to beat the two best teams to get to the finals. On Center Point's side they have placed the weakest teams in the district."

"Wonder who drew up that bracket?" William French asked as he leaned forward in the barber chair just in time for the barber to cut his left ear with the straight razor.

"I think it is pretty clear who did this. How does that school have so much power?" Henry, the barber, asked as he attempted to stop the bleeding on William's ear.

"I think it is pretty clear we will need to have a big crowd there every night from Crossroads, and we need to be ready to let them know that we are not going to take anything off of anyone," Rufus Green added. "I think we........"

"Now boys it's just a ball game," Coach Lester said as he interrupted Rufus. "I know you want to support the team, but we can't let our tempers outrun our sportsmanship."

"Sportsmanship, hell, coach we got nine boys that play their hearts out in every game, and we owe it to them to make sure the winner is decided on the court, not in someone's back pocket," Tyler Nelson responded with the head shaking approval of everyone in the barber shop.

"Now Tyler, if you want to support the boys, you leave that big double blade of yours at home. Last time you pulled that on the fans at Lead Hill, I got thrown out of the game," the coach said as all laughed as they recalled that event. "We will get things off and running Thursday night against

Ash Grove. We will see what happens after that."

"We'll just do our part to make sure there is an 'after that' if you don't mind," Henry said as he attempted to apologize to William and reassure him that he would not lose all of his ear.

Crossroads played their way past Ash Grove and Wild Cherry with two point victories in each game. Saturday night they faced Center Point in the finals for the district championship. It was a game that Center Point had bragged they would win at all cost.

The gym was full with Center Point fans taking as many of the bleachers as they could, forcing the Crossroads fans to stand at the ends of the gym.

A number of times during the first quarter Center Point players, coaches, and fans called on the refs to make the Crossroads fans move to give more room for the players. Those requests were always met with complaints from the Crossroads fans for more room in the bleachers for them.

"I tell you Henry, these refs are paid, and I sure didn't give them any money," Rufus said loud enough that Center Point fans and the refs could hear.

"You leave that off or you will be removed from this gym," one of the refs said as he walked toward Rufus.

"I know you Jacob Walker. You never called a game right in your life. You throw me out of this gym and I know the road you take home," Rufus replied.

"You Crossroads people just don't understand the rules to the game," came a cry from the bleachers. "We'll try to teach your children to read once we have your school."

"It'd be a cold day in hell before they have our school," Tyler told Henry. "I think I will just take my double blade and make my way up into that crowd and see if I can't find that guy."

"Thought the coach told you to leave that double blade at home. He didn't say anything to me about mine," Rufus responded as the two made their way up through the crowd.

"With this win we will consolidate," came the cry from the bleachers among the Center Point fans.

At that point the ref made a call none of the Crossroads fans could take, and most of the men and older boys took the court. The refs made their way to the Crossroads coaches and informed them that if they didn't get their fans off the court the game would be called and the victory given to Center Point.

After some time things settled down and the game continued. Center Point was leading Crossroads by six points, and it looked like they would win the game.

"Look at that, Joe," one of the players from the Crossroads team said. "They put your points up on the board on their side. Tell your dad that they are cheating us out of this game."

Joe ran by his dad on the next trip down the court and told him what Gene had seen. Johnny Mason made his way over to the coach's bench and checked the score. Sure as Joe had said, the score on the board did not agree.

At the next timeout Johnny Mason made his way to the center of the court and announced to the crowd that the folks from Center Point had grown up in a school system that did not teach their students how to count. He explained the correct score and said he would be working with the score keeper to make sure the score was correct for the rest of the game.

After a prolonged time of the refs trying to clear the floor and correct the game score, the game continued for the last quarter. It was at that time in the game that Samuel Mills began to hit his shots.

Every time down the court they got the ball to Samuel for a score. Every time the score keeper wrote the score on the board, Johnny made sure he saw his double blade and was ready to use it.

By the end of the game Crossroads had defeated the Center Point ball team. It was that team that went on to win the state championship. The following year the districts were redrawn and Crossroads never played Center Point again.

"It was the following year that Center Point began the process of working to have Crossroards consolidated into their school," Uncle Lee began to give his version of how that happened to Joe as he saw it.

"The following year Center Point ran one of their school board members for a key position at the state house. When he was elected he set to work to make sure that all of what he called 'smaller and inferior' schools be consolidated into the 'bigger and better' schools. He always used Crossroads and Center Point as his example," Uncle Lee explained. "The folks in Crossroads worked and raised money every year to improve the school, but no matter what they did certain folks at the state house always found fault with it. It took them six years, but they finally won and Crossroads lost it's school, all because of a ball game."

"Uncle Lee that is some story. I will say the folks around here are still serious about their basketball. I guess from what you say the school plays an important role in the life of these small towns. When they lose their schools they lose the thing that holds them together, that makes them community," Joe reasoned. "I got to be going. You look like you might need a nap. I noticed when I came in that you had a dog pen beside the house. I guess you used to hunt."

"I had foxhounds for years. Kept some of the best for miles around. Next time you come I will have to tell you about the biggest fox hunt ever held in this area," Uncle Lee said as he raised his hand to say farewell to Joe.

CHAPTER FIVE

THE FOX HUNT

During all the times that Joe had passed Uncle Lee's house on the summer bread route he had never seen an automobile parked at the home. Joe had developed the understanding in talking with Uncle Lee that he lived alone. This led to the conclusion that he never had visitors either. But as Joe drove into Uncle Lee's yard and saw the older model car parked close to the front porch, he realized that Uncle Lee would have needed someone to provide transportation for him. Even this older man who seemed content with very little would have needed food and other necessities.

This was probably a neighbor that provided those needs.

Joe closed the door on his car and walked to the porch to make sure it was okay for him to spend the afternoon with Uncle Lee. When he announced his presence the door opened and a beautiful young woman stood in the doorway. Uncommon for Joe, he could not take his eyes off this person, and for several minutes they made unbroken eye contact without a word being said. It was strange to Joe that this eye contact created a comfortable feeling, not the kind of feeling that Joe often had when he was dealing with people in difficult situations.

As comfortable as the feeling might have been, Joe still found himself struggling for just the right thing to say. He introduced himself and explained the reason for his visit. The young woman responded by letting him know that Uncle Lee was expecting him and that she had heard a great deal about him over the past few visits that she had made to check on Uncle Lee.

"Uncle Lee seems to think that you are a very special person, Joe Harrison," Mattie Haines said as she introduced herself. "I check on Uncle Lee a time or two each week to make sure he is okay and see if he needs anything. Guess you enjoy his stories from what he tells me."

Shocked by Mattie Haines' presence and natural beauty, Joe resorted to the oldest of topics in a situation like that and talked about the pretty day they were having and how weather changed so quickly in the Ozarks. Before he could think of anything else to say, Mattie excused herself and made her way to her car to leave.

"Good to meet you Mattie. I hope we can spend more time together," Joe said as he raised his voice to make sure she heard him.

Joe stood shocked at what he had just said. How could he have suggested that they should spend more time together? He didn't even know this person. She was probably married. Why did he have to say something like that?

Joe lost contact with the time and fact that he was standing on a porch in the Ozarks. His mind went back to the day he was walking across a parking lot in upper New York. There he saw a young woman in need of help carrying several packages that were too heavy for her to carry. Joe had rushed to her aid and encountered the most beautiful girl he had ever seen. Lost for words on that day Joe introduced himself by letting the girl know that he wasn't married.

Years had passed since that day and the young girl had become his wife. There had been too much water under the bridge of his life since that day for him to still find himself lost for words and make the statement he had just made to a stranger. However, the words had been spoken and he could not take them back.

"Are you coming in Joe Harrison?" came the voice from inside the house. It was Uncle Lee encouraging Joe to let his mind return to the present and come in for his afternoon visit. "Guess you met Mattie. She sure is a sweet person. I don't know what I would do without her help. I pay her as much as she will permit me to, but it certainly isn't as much as she needs with all the bills that she has."

Joe walked into the house to greet Uncle Lee and make some small talk before asking more specific questions about this new person, Mattie Haines.

"It is going to be a long, hard winter. I can feel it in my bones, and I don't think these old bones can take another one. We have been lucky for the past few years but there is something different about this year. You better ask as many questions as you can over the next few weeks. Course I'd guess that you might be making more than one trip a week this way if you knew that Mattie wasn't married. I am just going by that last statement you made to her. She lives about a mile up that dirt road south of the house," Uncle Lee said as he laid his head back in his rocker and closed his eyes as if he were drifting off into another place or time.

"I don't think you are having a good day. Do you want me to come back next week so that we can talk about that state wide fox hunt you mentioned last week?" Joe asked concerned that Uncle Lee's health was failing.

"No, just needed to catch my breath. I think it was in the early fall of '44 that our school was struggling for funds needed to make some repairs on the building. Ned Peel and I had fox hunted together for years when Ned came up with the idea to raise money for the school. Ned was one of those forward looking fellows that was always ahead of his time," Uncle Lee explained as he took Joe back to the night they made the plans for the hunt.

"You know Lee, I think ole' Dan'l is about the best foxhound in this county. I would say he would give any dog in the state a good race," Ned suggested.

Ole' Dan'l had just taken the lead in the chase as he always did when the fox made a turn up Slick Rock Creek and headed for Martha Evans' place. He seemed to know more about where the fox was going than the fox did in this area. Ned and Lee knew that the fox would take the hounds by Miss Evans' chicken house and through her barn yard before heading north over Piney Ridge and down Grapevine. It was always at that point that Ned would build a fire and the two men would talk about current events until the dogs came back into hearing across Wade Creek and up Sunny Slope to turn back toward Slick Rock.

"I have been thinking about a way we could help raise money for the school. It seems to me like a championship fox hunt might just do the trick. The hunters could camp on my forty by the school grounds. There is plenty of water at the spring. During the day they could eat at the school, and we could have the women bring in pies and cakes to sell. We could have games of horse shoes and even use the community baseball field for an old timer's game every afternoon. Late in the afternoon we could have a singing contest with the community band playing. Hell, we could have a major event here for a full week," Ned explained as he got carried away with his ability to come up with ideas.

"Listen to that ole' Dan'l would you," Lee interrupted. "He's almost got that fox by the tail. There's ole' Crockett right behind him. He's not going to be outrun tonight. He'll take the lead as they make their turn across Wade Creek."

"What do you think of my idea?" Ned continued. "You work with the school. Do you think they would go along with my idea? We would have to have their support to use the school grounds."

Within days the hunt was planned and the school was involved. Games to entertain the hunters during the day included horse shoes, a basketball game with the senior boys, and an old timers' baseball contest. Competition singing and entertainment from the community band was added. The school agreed to let out classes in the afternoon so that the students could enjoy some of the events.

"Well Lee, the only thing we need now is hunters. I sent out word all over the area and as far away as Little Rock. I told every-one that a price of twenty-five dollars would be given to any dog that could beat ole' Dan'l. I don't think you will need it, but you might want to make sure you have twenty-five dollars on Saturday night," Ned said as he looked at Lee with a look that suggested he might be serious.

"Why Ned, you know I have never had twenty-five dollars at one time in my life. I hope you have a back up plan for that money. You know ole' Dan'l hurt his leg last week," Uncle Lee replied in a very seri-ous tone.

Men came from all over in wagons and trucks to compete in the fox hunt and enjoy the daily events. The school provided meals for those who wanted to eat good cooking, and ball teams were formed along with male singing groups.

By Tuesday evening the groups had been drawn for the running of the hounds. The plans were to run on Tuesday evening and regroup for Thursday evening and again for Saturday evening so that the dogs would be running against different dogs each night. A final winner would be declared by the judges on Saturday night at the end of the run.

Wednesday and Friday nights were to be used to rest the dogs and have singing competition and a basketball game. Prizes were to be given to all winners of all the events.

By Wednesday morning news had spread across the communities that the Merryweather brothers from Wild Cherry were at the Crossroads School and would be singing in the competition that night. Their talent was known all over the Ozarks. No one had ever beaten them when they sang Rock of Ages or The Old Time Religion, and no one put the actions to I'll Fly Away like Bud and Albert Merryweather.

By late afternoon groups could be heard practicing all over the school grounds and camping area. Ned counted twelve different groups that had signed up to take part in the singing contest. Each group had at least one good lead singer. It was clear that people were in for one good evening of gospel singing.

The committee that had been created to plan and oversee the events had agreed not to charge for any of the activities. They had agreed that because of the difficult times that everyone who wanted to attend should be permitted to do so. The house would be full and many would have to stand around the outside of the building.

Group after group moved forward to showcase their talent. Some of the groups dressed up for the event and others wore overalls and plaid shirts. Some had musical instruments, some sang without instruments, and some asked the community band to play for them.

Each group seemed to create a following and an additional request for another song was common. It wasn't until four of the most common looking young men from Elmo Mountain began to sing that the entire crowd fell silent. The ability and seriouness with which they delivered their songs got the attention of everyone. By the time they had finished their last song everyone in the building was standing, and there wasn't a dry eye in the house. A winner had been found, and it was the Merryweathers who went forward to declare them the best they had ever heard.

The hunters had divided up for baseball teams and created a bracket for the afternoons. On Friday the team that had won the old timers' bracket played some of the high school boys from the school. The school administrators permitted the teachers to dismiss their classes and a serious game of baseball with all students from the school cheering their team on followed.

By the sixth inning it looked as though the old timers may have known more about the game than the high school boys, but their bodies just didn't have the ability to carry out what the minds suggested. They were willing to declare the high school players the winners after the seventh inning with suggestions being made that it would be a different story on the basketball court that night.

Friday night the gym was full of people from the community. The rumor had spread that the old timers had asked some of the boys who had played on championship teams around the area to join them for this game. Little did the old timers know that the senior boys from Crossroads had asked the state championship team of '42 to join them.

The old timers dressed in overalls and plaid shirts took little time to warm up and proclaim they were ready for action. When the seniors, dressed in ball suits, made their way on to the court everyone in the gym stood to give them their approval. It was easy to see that this was a home crowd, refs and all.

The game was played with the best sportsmanship ever shown at a basketball game in the Crossroads gym. For three quarters the lead changed back and forth between the two teams. It wasn't until the last three minutes of the game that the seniors managed to take a four-point lead and hold it to the end of the game.

As people left the gym that night most were talking about what a great week it had been. They were recalling the singing from Wednesday night and all the other events that they had enjoyed. It was certainly a sign of their approval of what had taken place at the school that week.

Ned and Lee talked on Saturday morning about what a great week it had been. They could not believe that a community could put that many hunters together for a week and not have disagreements with the judges and a good fight or two over something. If they could just make it through this last night of the running of the hounds they would pull off a major fund-raising event for the school. No doubt people would talk about them for some time as the two who saved the Crossroads school.

"Lee, it looks like your Dan'l dog has a real shot at winning this thing," Al Maxwell said as he walked up to Lee on Saturday night just before they turned their hounds loose for the last run. "You and Ned came up with a good idea in having this hunt. I hope you will consider making it a yearly thing."

"Ole' Dan'l has just been lucky I guess. You and some of the other fellows have the best hounds I have ever heard run," Lee responded in a polite voice. "Tonight will tell the story. We are going to be running over Slick Rock. There is a fox up there that has tricked about any dog ever run in that area."

Ned and Lee had saved the best area for the last night. This was their favorite area to run their dogs and they knew the area better than any other place. Lee was sure this would give ole' Dan'l the upper hand in winning the championship. He felt like this might be a little unfair, but he was willing to live with his feelings.

The judges explained the rules for one final time before the men turned their dogs loose. They wanted to make sure the hunters understood that they were to declare their dogs throughout the race. This meant that the hunters were to keep the judges informed on where their dogs were in the race and what they were doing. The hunters did this by telling the kind of bark their dogs were making.

The judges also explained that cutting and running would receive a deduction in points. Cutting and running was a sign the dog stopped barking to run faster so that it could get the lead, or was doing something else that wasn't acceptable. Little did any of the hunters know that this was to be the most interesting fox race ever run in this area.

Martha Evans had done her regular Saturday morning washing and hung her wash on the fence by the chicken house as she always did on Saturday morning. However, with all the activities at the school she had rushed off with her pie to help with lunch. She didn't realize that she had forgotten to take her wash down from the fence.

"That's ole' Dan'l taking the lead as they cross Slick Rock. He is running by smell, but he is on a fox," Lee explained to comply with the judge's rules.

"That's Shorty running behind him. He is running by scent," Andy Linn added.

"My dog, Rocky, is third, judge. He is running easy and sure of what he is after. It is a fox alright," Bill Thomas said.

"What are they doing now?" one of the judges ask. "I don't believe I have heard anything like this before. Have they caught the fox?"

As the fox took the dogs through Martha Evans' barn-yard, Crockett ran into some of Martha's night clothing. Tangled in the mess, some of the other dogs treed him and a fight followed for a few minutes.

"That's ole' Dan'l taking the fox north toward Piney Ridge. He's after the fox. I don't know what the other dogs are doing," Lee suggested in a manner of speaking to defend his dog's ability to keep on the trail.

"Well, that's my dog Rocky heading south and he is after a fox. I don't know what has happened to his bark, but he doesn't run trash," Bill Thomas said in a defensive tone.

"I don't know about your dogs," Andy Linn interrupted. "Shorty has the fox and he is headed east toward the Persimmon Pond. I know that area, and my dog will take him around the pond and bring him back this way."

Other hunters began an effort at explaining what their dogs might be doing, but for some reason the dogs had split up and races were taking different directions from Martha Evans' barnyard.

Now it just happened that Buddy Fields owned a farm on the Persimmon Pond. Saturday evening was his favorite time of the week. It was on this evening that Buddy enjoyed sitting on his front porch tasting the week's brew. He did this to make sure it would be of the quality necessary to sell to the local folks over at Missionary Ridge the following week.

On different occasions, after a few drinks, Buddy had seen ghosts walking around in the Persimmon Pond Cemetery a hundred and fifty yards up the road from his porch. But of all things on this night, there was one in his barnyard.

Shorty had run through one of Martha Evans' long night gowns and was tangled in it in such a way that it waved in the wind when he ran. As Shorty entered Buddy's barnyard, a raccoon ran up a fence post and Shorty, interested in raccoons, began jumping up and down trying to catch the raccoon.

Buddy quickly found his double barrel shotgun that he kept close at hand and moved toward the barnyard. Afraid to get too close, he fired both barrels at the white moving object and filled Martha Evans' best gown full of shot. This permitted Shorty to free himself from the gown and with the shots being fired in his direction, he made a run for the point where the judges had the hunters turn their dogs loose.

In the meantime Rocky was taking his race south toward James Hardin's farm. James had lost a son in the war and had begun to create his own understanding of reality. He was sure the war would not end until the foreigners came to America and killed everyone. He thought that the Ozarks would be the first place they would take, so he was prepared for the attack.

Rocky had run though some of Martha's under clothing and had an object caught in his mouth. This changed the tone of his bark but didn't slow his effort at whatever he was chasing. James was awakened by the strange bark and quickly alerted his wife to the fact that the enemy had already turned their foreign dogs loose on their place and would be coming to take them at any time.

James Hardin rushed to his front porch and began firing in all directions. This was enough distraction to cause Rocky to give up his effort at chasing whatever he was after and drop out.

Within an hour most of the dogs had returned to their owners except ole' Dan'l.

He was running some race and Lee was calling it as if he were with the dog and knew every move he was making.

After two hours the judges attempted to call the hunt. They wanted to send the hunters back to camp and declared that they needed some time to discuss what had just happened. All the hunters had suggestions about what should be done but none seemed to agree. It was clear that each dog owner wanted a decision that favored his dog.

There wasn't going to be an agreeable conclusion to this fox hunt. Every hunter was already convinced that Ned and Lee had saved this last area to run because they knew what the outcome would be.

By the time the judges got the hunters back to camp hard words were being said, and it looked like punches might be thrown before the men were willing to settle down. What had been a great week of fellowship was just about to turn into an all-out-brawl, and all because of a little misunderstanding about what might have happened at Martha Evans' barnyard.

Since Ned was the polished speaker in the group, Lee encouraged him to step forward and work out some kind of a solution.

This Ned agreed to do as Lee pushed him forward into the center of the group.

After a rather long discussion, everyone agreed that ole' Dan'l had been the best dog in the races the first two nights. Slowly the group began to accept the fact that he was the only dog to work through whatever happened in the barnyard and stay with what was believed to be a fox. This finally led to the conclusion that ole' Dan'l should be declared the winner of the fox hunt, but that the title champion should be withheld for lack of a clear winner.

Since it was almost daylight before a solution was reached, Sunday morning's singing and worship service was called off. Most hunters packed up their gear and left for home. Ned didn't think there was much need to remind them of the Christmas dance that they would be holding at the school later in the year, but he attempted to do so anyway.

"Now Joe, that fox hunt was discussed for years in these parts and beyond," Uncle Lee said as he looked at Joe to see if he had any questions. "Yes sir, ole' Dan'l was a clear champion of the best fox hounds that ever ran these ridges or any ridges for miles around."

CHAPTER SIX

THE LAST CHRISTMAS DANCE

Joe had planned on driving around the Elbow community when he left Uncle Lee's, but his story of the fox hunt had taken so long that it was almost dark when he left his house. Of course, the area he intended to look at was south of Uncle Lee's house about a mile down the dirt road.

After losing his wife and children in the automobile accident in New York, Joe had decided that he would never consider marriage again. His introduction to Mattie Haines had caused him to give second thought to that decision.

One thing that Uncle Lee had said about Mattie kept running through his mind. What did he mean by all the bills that she had? He needed more information about who she was and the kind of life that she lived. She did not give the appearance to Joe of being a person that would try to live beyond her means.

Joe had not suggested another day that he would return to visit with Uncle Lee. He had observed that Uncle Lee wasn't well. Therefore, as bad as he wanted more information about the history of Elbow, he thought it might be a good idea to give him some time to rest. The visits seemed to take a lot out of the ninety-six year old man. Besides, he had work at his place that needed to be done before the cold weather.

Over the weekend Joe's mind returned to his encounter with Mattie. He wasn't familiar enough with the area to know of anyone that might give him the information he wanted. After all, as Jake had said many times, folks in the Ozarks just do not pry into the lives of others.

On Tuesday Joe decided to drive into Turnbow and order some of the materials he needed for the work on his house.

While in Turnbow Joe had a list of things he needed from the grocery store. This meant an encounter with Mrs. Dobbins, but these were things he had to have.

"Good morning Mrs. Dobbins," Joe said as he entered the store. "I have a list I need some help with."

"Why certainly Joe. I haven't seen you around in some time. Have you been ill?"

"No, I have been visiting an individual by the name of Uncle Lee over at Elbow. He is helping me with the history of his area," Joe responded.

"I've heard that name. I didn't know he was still living. He must be almost one hundred years old," Mrs. Dobbins replied.

"He's ninety-six according to what he says. He is a very interesting person. He has a good mind, but tells the history from his perspective I think," Joe said.

"Does he live alone? The best I remember all of his family died years ago," Mrs. Dobbins asked looking at Joe with a concerned look.

"He lives alone, but a Mattie Haines checks on him several times a week. She makes sure he has food to eat," Joe explained.

"Mattie Haines! Why I know Mattie. She buys her groceries here. That is why she buys more than one person could eat. I have wondered about that. She is taking some of the food to him," Mrs. Dobbins said in a tone that suggested that she was beginning to figure out a puzzle that had been bothering her. "She's such a nice girl. You would never have guessed that she had a town drunk for a father."

"I guess I don't know that much about the history of the people in this area. Jake always told me that I shouldn't ask questions about the personal lives of people in this area," Joe said.

"And you shouldn't Joe. It's just that everyone knew about Gene Haines. He was considered the biggest drunk, cheat, and liar in the whole county. He got in fights everywhere he went. Some folks said he killed a man in a knife fight over in Mortonville for two dollars. Not that I am saying anything that everyone doesn't already know. He owed just about everyone money when he died. They tell me that this poor girl is working at all kinds of jobs so that she can pay off her father's debts. She's such a sweet thing," Mrs. Dobbins said as she was interrupted by the telephone which gave Joe an opportunity to escape.

As Joe left the grocery store he was more than concerned about the fact that Jake had always told him not to pry into people's personal lives. It seemed to him that Mrs. Dobbins knew too much about Gene Haines and was willing to share it with just about anyone. At least he had learned her version of Mattie's background. The father's side, anyway.

The information about the Haines family did leave Joe with one question. Why would Mattie work so hard to pay off debts that had been created by her father if he was such a bad person? Joe thought Uncle Lee might have the answer to that question, but then there was this Ozark rule of staying out of people's personal lives. Of course, if he just brought up the subject and Uncle Lee shared as freely as Mrs. Dobbins, there wouldn't be anything wrong with that.

Joe made his way back over to the lumber yard to see if they would be able to deliver his material by Wednesday. That would give him the rest of the week to work on his house, and it would give Uncle Lee a week to rest.

On his way home, Joe met a car that looked just like the one Mattie was driving the day he saw her at Uncle Lee's place. As he cleared his head, he decided that he just had her on his mind and was seeing things. He had to turn his attention to other issues. She wasn't that important and besides Uncle Lee had said that several young men had tried to gain her affection and all had failed. Maybe she was the kind of person who just wasn't interested in men.

Joe didn't believe in God, not since he had lost his wife and children in the auto accident. It seemed to him that all the goodness folks talked about didn't match the experiences he dealt with in life. He did try to respect Sunday and had made a decision not to work on that day. He used it for rest and planning the following week's work.

Monday was a pretty day, warmer than usual for that area of the country at that time of year. Joe was thinking that Uncle Lee might be wrong about a bad winter, and he might get to complete all the jobs he had on his list. However, the day was so pretty that Joe could not take his mind off the kind of story Uncle Lee might have ready for him if he drove over to Elbow. And, of course, there was Mattie. She was on Joe's mind also.

By lunch, with his mind on other things, Joe gave up and drove to Elbow. To his pleasant surprise Mattie's car was parked in

Uncle Lee's yard. He had hoped that would be the case.

"I guess you make smooth talk to women but don't intend to keep your word," Mattie greeted Joe as he got out of his car. "Thought you said you looked forward to spending more time with me. I didn't respond to that statement when you said it, but maybe I can save you time and trouble by letting you know that I don't have time for what men are interested in."

"Well, I haven't been in the Ozarks that long, but I hadn't noticed that women are so outspoken around here," Joe answered. "Don't you have to get to know a man before you know what his interests are?"

"Been around enough men over the past four years to know that they are all looking for the same thing," Mattie responded as she walked to her car. "Uncle Lee isn't feeling well today. You might want to cut your visit short."

"Thank you for the advice. Maybe after my visit I will have time to drive over to your place and see what takes up so much of your time," Joe answered with a tone of dissatisfaction over how Mattie had responded to him.

"That's just like a man alright. They are always willing to watch a woman work. I have never had one to suggest that they had time to come over and help me do part of the work I do," Mattie got in her car and slammed the door to drive off. It was at that point that she discovered the battery was low and would not start her car.

"Of course, I am just one of those men who likes to stand and watch women work, but I do have some cables in the back of my car if you would like to use them," Joe said. "I think I can get them for you if you are the kind of woman who is willing to accept help."

"Okay! It has been a bad day for me. If it is okay with you, I would like for you to help me start my car. I have a lot to do," Mattie answered in a low defeated tone.

"Mattie Haines, it would be my pleasure to help you with your car," Joe said in a low tone to suggest that he wasn't taking pride in having the last word in this situation.

Mattie thanked Joe for his help. Joe could see that she had tears in her eyes and didn't need any more negative statements from him. He struggled for something to say that would be more positive in nature.

"I don't know much about farm work, but I do have some extra time on my hands. If there is anything that I can ever do to help,

I would like for you to permit me to do so. When I help a woman I don't expect anything in return," Joe said to Mattie as he made eye contact to let her know that he was serious about the offer.

Joe walked to the porch and called to Uncle Lee to let him know that he was in the yard. He was greeted with a weak voice asking him to come in that he had been expecting him.

"That Mattie Haines is a rather strange woman," Joe said to Uncle Lee as he walked into the room. "I guess I don't really know that much about women, but she's not like others I have known."

"She has more to deal with than most other women. Maybe that is what makes her different," Uncle Lee suggested.

"Do you know much about her?" Joe asked.

"About as much as anyone I reckon. I have known her from the day she was born," Uncle Lee explained.

"I was over at a store in Turnbow the other day and a person in the store had some bad things to say about her father," Joe told Uncle Lee.

"I would guess most folks would have bad things to say about Gene Haines. I would say he might have been the most misunderstood person in the county," Uncle Lee suggested.

"Sounds like you knew him pretty well," Joe responded.

"He died on that bed about four or five years ago. Came in here about two in the morning. It had been raining and freezing most of the night. Some fellows at Mortonville had worked him over pretty good. The beating and long walk through the rain and cold was more than his body could take. I tried to help him but he died the next morning. Seems like everyone had something against him," Uncle Lee told Joe.

"I was told that he was a drunk, cheat, and liar. Is that not so?" Joe asked hoping that it might not be true for Mattie's sake.

"Oh, he was a drunk alright. But he was also a hard worker and a loving father. No one could have loved a child more than he did Mattie. Folks learned that they could get him drunk and then claim that he was trying to cheat them just to get a fight started," Uncle Lee explained. "People been taking advantage of Mattie over money they claim he owed them ever since his death, and she is just good enough to try to pay it back."

"You mean she may be paying folks money she doesn't even owe them?" Joe asked with a raised tone of voice suggesting that he was upset that people might be taking advantage of her.

"I'd say he owed the money alright, but I don't think she should be concerned about paying it back. They all got enough out of Gene to make up any loss they claim. This all started at a Christmas dance they had at the school in '45.

"How could a Christmas dance in 1945 have anything to do with Gene Haines and Mattie?" Joe asked.

In the fall of 1945 the Crossroads school board met to consider a request from the community to use the gym for a Christmas dance. The gym had been used in the past, but several members of different churches had asked the board to turn down any future request because of the drinking and fights that had taken place at past events.

The board was divided over the issue but finally agreed to let the community have the gym if they would be willing to police the event and make sure that no fights occurred. The committee that had been established to oversee the dance selected six young men that they thought could handle any problems that might occur.

Buddy Fields from Persimmon Pond had always provided the special brew for events like the dance, but he had promised that he would not for this dance since it was on Christmas. However, he hadn't promised that he would not sell his brew to anyone who might come by his place on the way to the dance.

"I was one of the men asked to police the dance that year," Uncle Lee told Joe. "I wasn't that young, but I had always played a role in school events, and I was going to be playing in the band at the dance. The committee said I was well respected and should have more influence over the older men than anyone they knew."

"But Uncle Lee what did that dance have to do with Mattie?" Joe asked.

"I'm getting to that, but you have to have the whole story. It all started at that dance. Gene Haines was the best looking man anywhere in these parts at that time. Young women, married or not, wanted to dance with him during the dances. The two prettiest young women in the county were Betty Fields and Cora Mae Weathers. They seemed to take great pleasure in getting

THE LAST CHRISTMAS DANCE

men all worked up and fighting over them. At the Christmas dance they both set out to get Gene Haines. One would dance with him and then the other would cut in until they were almost fighting each other to hold on to Gene," Uncle Lee explained as he laid his head back in his chair to rest and let his mind go back to that night of the dance.

"Gene said he would walk me home after the dance," Betty Fields bragged to Cora Mae as they walked to the side of the gym together to rest.

"Oh, he did did he, well we will just see about that. After this next dance I will have him agreeing to anything I want him to do and that will include walking me home," Cora Mae responded in an angry tone.

"Gene, I have some of that good brew you like in my coat," Cora Mae said as they danced. "If you will walk me home I will share it with you."

"I can't Cora Mae. I promised Betty I would walk her home, besides she brought some of her father's good stuff to drink," Gene responded.

"Betty, why Gene don't you know about her? You walk her home and you will be the father of that baby she is carrying," Cora Mae said.

"Baby! she didn't say anything about a baby. Whose baby is it?" Gene asked.

"Well, no one knows for sure. She has been with so many different boys, but some say it is Ike Martin's," Cora Mae suggested.

"Ike Martin, hell he doesn't even know Betty. How could he be the father?" Gene said.

"Well, Betty does have a way of getting around. But if you will walk me home you won't regret it. Just tell Betty you have changed your mind. She has plenty of other boys waiting to take her home," Cora Mae added.

Instead of Gene taking Cora Mae's word about Betty, he went to her and asked if she was carrying Ike Martin's baby. It just happened that Bobby Vines overheard Gene and quickly told several of the other fellows that Gene said that Ike had been seeing Betty and she was having his baby.

By the time the word got over the dance floor to Ike, it was told in such a way that Gene had accused Ike of getting Betty pregnant, and he was going to take care of Ike for doing that to his girl. Ike had been hitting the brew pretty hard that evening and he was spoiling for a fight. This was just what he needed because he had been told that his girl friend had been seeing Gene.

With the help of several people at the dance who enjoyed encouraging fights at these events, sides began to develop and a fight broke out inspite of the committee's effort to stop it. Since Gene was so good looking and all the girls wanted to date him, all the boys pitched in to change his looks.

The committee's inability to stop the fight let both men and women get involved. Before long a great deal of damage was done to the gym and the Christmas dance was over.

"Uncle Lee, are you saying that it was because of Gene's looks that people always picked on him over the years?" Joe asked.

"Well, that was the beginning of it. It seemed that after that night everywhere Gene went boys continued to take out their anger on him because of their jealousy. Stories were always told on him that he was seeing men's wives and the babies being born might be his," Uncle Lee told.

"Was there any truth to all those stories?" Joe asked.

"Might have been in the beginning, but once he married Betty that was the end of his running around," Uncle Lee explained.

"You mean he married Betty Fields? That would mean that Mattie is Buddy Field's granddaughter," Joe said, shocked at what he had heard. "I thought Cora Mae said she was pregnant."

"No truth to that. Once Gene found out that Cora Mae was not telling the truth, he married the girl he really loved," Uncle Lee said.

"What happened to Betty? You said Mattie lived alone. Betty shouldn't be that old," Joe said.

"She left Gene about three years before he died for Ike Martin," Uncle Lee answered with a strange look on his face.

"Ike Martin, the one at the Christmas dance?" Joe asked.

"The same one. She told after Gene died that she had been seeing Ike all the years she was married. I guess that was the truth," Uncle Lee said.

"Why did she marry Gene if she loved Ike?" Joe wanted to know.

"She said she married him to get even with Cora Mae for the story she told on her at the dance," Uncle Lee responded.

"I've got to be on my way. This is the most unusual story you have told yet. I am going to have to give a great deal of thought to it. Somewhere in the middle of all of this is

Mattie, and I am sure there is a story about her also," Joe suggested.

"Mattie is a fine young lady who is paying for the sins of her folks. In spite of that, she is a keeper as we would say about an outstanding fox hound. The hound that can catch her will certainly be a state champion, Joe Harrison," Uncle Lee said as Joe stood to leave.

On Wednesday Joe was back in Turnbow picking up more supplies and getting a hair cut at the barber shop. The barber had the ability to pry into one's past without pushing so far that it offended the person, but Joe was careful to only share what he wanted him to know.

As Joe finished his turn in the chair, he thanked Max for a good hair cut and suggested that he needed to drop by the grocery store to pick up some items.

"Be careful because Cora Mae has a way of being nosy about people's personal lives. You don't want to tell her too much because she has a way of adding to what you say," Max warned Joe with a chuckle.

CHAPTER SEVEN

STELLA'S BOARDING HOUSE

Uncle Lee will be back out under those Oak trees on a day like this, Joe thought to himself as he drove toward Elbow. Uncle Lee hadn't been feeling very well the last time or two that Joe had visited him, but today was a mild day for October and Joe knew that he would be better today.

A mile or so before Joe reached the road that turned into Uncle Lee's yard a car that Joe didn't recognize stopped in the road and two men flagged him down. The two men just a little younger than Joe got out of their car and walked over to Joe's car. They were good-sized men who seemed bent on doing some kind of harm, but ten years earlier

Joe had been 'all everything' in high school sports in New York. He had also grown up in an area where boys had to learn to fight to survive. With all the training he had received he had learned to take care of himself. So while he was curious as to what these men might want, he wasn't afraid of them.

"You been asking questions about Mattie Haines, mister?" one of the individuals asked as he put his hand on the door to Joe's car.

"I thought the folks in the Ozarks minded their own business," Joe replied in a clear tone that suggested he was willing to stand his ground.

"My friend asked you a question mister. It would be a good idea for you to answer it," the other stranger said as he moved along-side his friend.

"I gave you the only answer you are going to get, but I am willing to put it in a way that you can better understand it. Get in your damn car and get out of my way or I will beat the hell out of both of you," Joe said raising his voice but still showing control and confidence in his ability to do just what he said he would do.

"Mister, you are asking for more trouble than you can handle. You outsiders have to be taught to mind your own business. You leave Mattie Haines alone or it won't be good for you. You got that?" The bigger of the two men said.

"I am on my way to see Mattie now," Joe answered. "But let me give the two of you some good advice. You forget whatever you think your interest is in Mattie, and I won't have to teach you to mind your own business, got it!"

Joe drove on over to Uncle Lee's. He hadn't made any plans to visit Mattie but with the run-in he had just experienced, he thought maybe he would.

Joe was right about Uncle Lee. As he approached the trees he could see the rocking chair and the old man sitting in the chair dressed in his overalls and plaid shirt. It was a pretty day and Joe guessed that Uncle Lee wanted to enjoy all of them he could.

"Thought I might find you out here today. You must be feeling better," Joe said as he got out of his car.

"Feel some better I guess. We don't have many days like this, so I wanted to enjoy as much of it as I can," Uncle Lee answered.

" I got stopped by two men in an old blue Ford car back down the road. They suggested that I shouldn't be seeing Mattie. Do you know who they might have been, or what interest they have in Mattie?" Joe asked.

"That would be James Dobbins and Bud Fields I reckon," Uncle Lee answered. "Bud may be related to Mattie in some way, and James has run after her for the past year or two."

"Would James be related to Mrs. Dobbins that runs the store over at Turnbow?" Joe asked.

"I guess he would be her son. Not too sure about that however. I do know that they are trouble. Bud supplies the brew from his makings on the mountain, and they spend their time bothering as many people as they can."

"Is Bud related to the Buddy Fields that you told me about some time back?" Joe asked.

"He is related some way, but I am not sure how. The Fields were all related by having children from several women they weren't married to," Uncle Lee explained. "Just be careful because they can be trouble."

"I told them that I was on my way over to see Mattie today. I think after we visit a while I'll keep that promise," Joe said.

"Didn't take you for the kind of person who would be scared off of something you wanted. I guess you would like to hear about Stella Jordon. She was that kind of person. She sure bluffed the people in Crossroads while she was here," Uncle Lee told Joe.

Stella's boarding house was the large building in town that looked completely out of place in Crossroads. It was three stories high and had open hallways on every level. The windows looked like those in costly houses in New England. It was clear from the design of the building that the person who had drawn up the plans wasn't interested in creating something that fit into the common designs of buildings in Crossroads.

"Stella came to Crossroads about '43 I reckon. People tried to find out where she was from, but she didn't share much of her past. She just blew into town one day with a lot of money and bought the land the boarding house sets on. It wasn't long until she had a group of outsiders camping on the land and building her boarding house," Uncle Lee explained. "The local stores couldn't supply all of her needs, so she had material brought in as far away as Chicago and large cities back in the east. That was the first thing that upset the local people."

"Now, by boarding house are you talking about a place for the high school students who came to school here to stay? You said students boarded with local folks around town." Joe interrupted.

"The School Improvement Society was hoping that was what she had in mind, but it didn't work out that way. The Improvement Society was made up of several women from the area who made and carried out plans to improve the school. They went over one day to meet with Stella to see what she had in mind," Uncle Lee explained.

"I don't think I have ever visited anyone living in a tent before," Clara, president of the School Improvement Society, said as the group walked across the property purchased by Stella for her boarding house. "Looks like all the men are keeping their places pretty clean."

"I tell you Clara, I don't understand a single woman living among so many men. There must be something wrong with this that we can't see," Sara explained as she looked around at all the workers.

"Some of these men don't look very old. I wonder if they have families?" Jane added.

"Well, have you ever seen the like," Clara exclaimed as she walked into Stella's tent. "Look at all the art work and ....Oh my! They are all young, naked women. Why would she want pictures like this?"

"Oh, Clara look at this one," Jane said as she walked over to one of the paintings. "Would you look at what that young woman is doing with that man?"

"Ladies, I think we have our answer without even talking to Miss Stella Jordan," Sara added as she turned to leave the tent.

It was at that time Stella walked into the tent to greet the women. Stella was dressed in clothing that only the rich could afford. She spoke in a polite tone with the language of a Southern bell until one of the members of the society expressed concern about the paintings.

It didn't take Stella long to let them know that it was none of their business. However, they quickly learned that it wasn't high school students she was interested in. She was planning for high paying boarders who wanted to spend a few nights and enjoy their stay," Uncle Lee explained.

The women of the School Improvement Society took it upon themselves to quickly spread what they had learned from Stella Jordon. They made sure the men of the town who had organized as a 'moral society' knew about what Stella had told them. These men had taken it upon themselves to be responsible for dealing with people who did not meet the moral standards of the town.

On different occasions, these men had visited homes in the night to leave signs that warned men who were abusing their wives or children. They also dealt with women who were not faithful to their husbands or husbands who might be roaming the area when they should be at home.

It also just happened that the chicken peddler was in town and collected all the information being told by the society. Truman Gardner had run a chicken route all over the area for years. He bought chickens or traded a limited number of items that he carried on the back of his 1937 truck for chickens. He had become known far and wide as the chicken peddler. But his main reputation was known as the person who carried news of events from one area of the country to the other.

Children gathered wherever Truman's truck was seen to listen to his stories. Adults gathered to listen to Truman share the news in only the way he could. Most realized that his version of the news wasn't the actual truth, but they listened with great interest anyway.

The one thing everyone could be certain about was that Truman Gardner would change the story about Stella Jordon a number of times. By the time he was through with the story, men would be coming from far and wide to see Stella and her boarding house.

Great concern about what the chicken peddler would tell about the boarding house caused the town's folks to look for someone to come up with a solution. When the men of the 'moral society' saw that most of the people in the area only intended to talk about what was being built in their town but didn't intend to do anything about it, they decided to act.

"I think we should pay a visit to this Stella Jordon now before she gets too far along with her boarding house," one member of the 'moral society' said.

"Sounds like a good idea to me. If we permit her to get too far along with this building, it may be difficult for us to convince her to leave town," another member of the group agreed.

"I would say dropping by late tonight with a good large bundle of switches should do the job. We will place them in front of her property with a note letting her know she's not going to build a boarding house for what she has in mind in Crossroads," a third member of the group suggested.

That night some of the men of the group carried out their plan. The following day people coming into town from the community to shop were shocked to see how Stella had responded. The switches had been placed in the ground along the road and hanging on each switch was a piece of Stella's underwear. Most of these men in the area had never seen a display like this of such personal items.

It looked like this lesson had not worked as planned, and the society quickly met to create new plans. Some of the members suggested that they make a second visit and use one or two of the switches on Stella. They had done that a time or two in the past and it had always worked. Other members suggested that they use a bucket of syrup and a pillow case full of feathers.

They thought that might convince her to give up the project.

Before the group could take a final vote on the ideas, Tommy reminded them that Stella had according to his count, fifteen men working for her. He had noticed during the morning that these men seemed to be setting up some form of line for protection around the building. According to what he had seen, he wasn't sure a second visit was a good idea.

With that new information, the group decided to ask the pastors from the churches in town to make a visit and see if they could talk to Stella. After all, the moral responsibility of the area did belong to the pastors. That was what the society decided that they paid the preachers to do.

The ministers met to discuss possible solutions to the problem that everyone in town seemed concerned about. They had learned that the town did not have any rules against such a building that Stella intended to build. The only way that this project could be stopped was for the ministers to visit Stella and present the Gospel to her in such a way that she would repent of her evil intentions and build something acceptable to the town.

The ministers decided to present their findings to their churches on Sunday and ask all members to be in prayer for them as they made their visit at one o'clock on Monday. With everyone in town praying at that hour, they were sure that they would be successful in changing Stella's intentions.

Brother Harold of the First Church was selected as the spokesman for the group. He was to lead the meeting with Stella on Monday. All the other ministers had agreed that he was the proper choice for such an important mission. After all, he had been successful in winning some of the most difficult drunks in the area over the years.

"Miss Jordon the ministers of the town have come to talk with you about your plans for this building," Brother Harold said as he entered Stella's tent on Monday afternoon. "We are deeply concerned that your boarding house will bring sin to our community that our young people should not see."

"I guess sin is a relative term, sir," Stella quickly responded. "I have read the Bible you preach from, and it seems to me that my kind of building was common throughout what you call the Old Testament. Even the people that proclaimed themselves to be your God's best enjoyed many wives and other women."

"Well now, Miss Jordon, it is clear you have read the Bible, but it seems you have read it with the interpretation you wanted it to have," Brother Harold responded. "There is another part to the Bible called the New Testament, you know."

"Oh, yes, the New Testament, that part that talks about Jesus eating and keeping company with women like me," Stella interrupted. "I guess that would mean that you men should make yourselves right at home in my tent. You might want to walk around and enjoy the wonderful art work I have collected. Why, sit down and let me wash your feet with some of my best oils and maybe just a tear or two."

"Now Miss Jordon, we have the entire town praying at this very hour that you will hear the Gospel from our perspective. I think it is clear you know enough about the Bible to know that you need to repent and give up this plan you have. The folks here in Crossroads want you to be an accepted part of town," Brother Harold explained.

"You mean accepted as long as I do things to please them," Stella said. "I may go to your hell when I die, but as long as

I am living, I intend to do things to please myself. Now, if you have said your piece I would guess that all your fine folks in town are through praying, so I will say good day to you fine gentlemen."

"I don't think I have seen anyone as cold hearted as that woman," one of the ministers said as they left Stella's tent.

"It will take a lot of prayer to change that one," another one said.

"Just remember our God is bigger than Stella Jordon. When the time is right, He will have his way with her," Brother Harold said.

"What do we do in the meantime? This building will be completed before long, and men will be coming to visit our town," one said.

"You may be forgetting that she will be bringing other young women to the boarding house. I tell you we have a real problem on our hands," another minister suggested.

"I have a solution to this. We will meet with our members and establish a prayer time. Day and night we will have people around this property praying for Stella," Brother Harold answered.

"That will work Brother Harold," they all agreed.

"We may want to start with the women of the churches. I am not sure some of the men need this kind of temptation right now," the pastor from the Faith First Church suggested.

The churches in Crossroads joined together to fight the sin that was coming to their town. Prayer groups were set up so that members of the different churches were near the property of Stella's at most hours of the day and night.

Some groups called for God to send fire and destroy the evil that was being built. Others called for God to convert Stella so that her money could be used in the town for good projects. But no matter how the people prayed, the building was completed and the men took up their tents and moved on.

Stella placed a large sign announcing that the boarding house would be open for business on a specific day. At that announcement the prayer groups disbanded, and it looked like Crossroads was going to have a house of sin whether they wanted it or not.

"I came by the boarding house this morning and it looked to me like something had changed," Clara told some of the members of the School Improvement Society.

"I noticed something different, but I couldn't figure out what it was," another member said.

"Well, I don't want to be one accused of starting rumors, but I heard last night that Stella Jordon left town," Jane told the group.

"Left town! Why would she have left town?" Clara asked.

"I don't know but the pastor from Faith First Church is missing also. His wife said he just up and left," Jane answered.

"With that, the boarding house was closed for business. The members of the Faith First Church later disbanded because they did not have a pastor. It was said that you could hear some of the churches in town praising God for answering their prayers. I'm not sure it was God who answered their prayers, but the town didn't have to deal with Stella's boarding house, that was for sure," Uncle Lee concluded.

"You're telling me that Stella just up and left town and no one ever knew what happened to her. That doesn't make sense," Joe said.

"Well, Brother Harold kept telling the folks in town that God works in strange ways. I guess He could have used the pastor from Faith. That would have been strange alright," Uncle Lee told Joe as he laughed.

"What did the town do with the boarding house?" Joe asked.

"After a year or two some of the folks decided to use it to board high school students who came here from other communities. They moved all the art work to the third floor and boarded male students on the first two floors. Some said you could see lamp lights late at night moving around on the third floor. I guess the students must have been studying art," Uncle Lee concluded. "Anyway, the building was used to house students until the school was closed. It hasn't been used for anything since."

"Uncle Lee, I have got to tell you that is the strangest story you have told yet. It's not that late, so I think I will drive down the road and see if Mattie is home," Joe said.

"Be careful now Joe, don't start anything you don't intend to finish. Be sure to drop back by when you can, I am sure you will want to know about the gravestone in the cemetery," Uncle Lee said as he stood to walk back to his house.

Joe drove down the road a short distance when he saw a car like Mattie's on the side of the road. It looked like a person was attempting to change a tire on the car.

"Well, hello Mattie Haines, it looks like every time we meet you have car trouble. I have never had the opportunity to watch an independent woman change a tire before. Do you mind if I just sit here on the fender of my car and watch?" Joe said as he got out of his car and leaned on his car door.

"Why, no Joe Harrison, that is just what I would expect any male to do! I'm sorry that I do not have anything to eat or drink to offer you, but maybe my effort at changing this tire will be entertainment enough," Mattie responded in a very unfriendly tone.

"While you work on that tire, I might share an experience I had on my way over to Uncle Lee's today. I met two young men that seemed to have some interest in you. I believe their names were Bud Fields and James Dobbins," Joe explained to Mattie as she stopped working on the tire and turned with a concerned look to see what Joe had to say. "I told you Mattie, I am not like other men you have had to deal with. They don't scare me, and I can promise you that they won't bother you. Now if you will let me, I will change that flat tire for you."

Joe changed the tire as Mattie broke down and shared some of the problems she had experienced with Bud Fields and James Dobbins. Joe reassured her that he was capable of dealing with the two of them if she would permit him to get involved. By the end of their conversation, Mattie had decided that she had found a person in Joe Harrison that she could trust, at least she was willing to give it a try.

CHAPTER EIGHT

FANCY BURGER'S FUNERAL (THE GRAVESTONE)

By the first of November Joe had completed just about all the house repair projects he had on his list. He had also written several chapters on his book of unusual stories from the Ozarks. With Uncle Lee supplying so much information, that had not been a difficult task.

The fall had seen radical weather changes. Some days would be warmer than usual while other days were cold with heavy rain. There had been major storms in some parts of the Ozarks with these changes, but the Turnbow area had been spared. On this particular day it was too cold to work outside, and Joe had not visited Uncle Lee or Mattie for several days, so he decided to forgo any work and gather more information for his book.

On the way to Elbow Joe remembered that Uncle Lee had suggested he would tell him about the gravestone in the cemetery, so he thought he would stop by and look the stone over. It stood out as an unusual stone in the front of the cemetery, certainly difficult to miss as one drove by.

Joe stopped at the entrance to the cemetery and sat in his car for a time looking at all the markers across the land. It was a large cemetery with a large number of graves. Joe could tell by the shape and condition of many of the stones that it had existed for many years. It gave proof to what Uncle Lee had said about the town. At one time Elbow, or Crossroads, had to be a rather large town for that area of the Ozarks.

Joe walked from his car to the front gate and paused to take a closer look at the gravestone Jake had found so interesting. Finally, Joe walked around the stone just a little puzzled at its structure. He could tell the marker had been assembled by people who had a great interest in the person in that grave. But as Jake had said, it was surely one of a kind.

As Joe started to leave something about the marker caught his eye. There was a date of death on the marker, but it did not have a date of birth. Why would they leave that information off the stone? He was sure Uncle Lee would have the answer.

Too cold for Uncle Lee to be outside, Joe found him in the house wrapped in a quilt sitting in his rocker. This caused Joe to look more closely at the room. There was a fire in the wood stove but the house was still cold. There wasn't any protection on the windows, and different areas of the house looked as though they didn't have that much protection on the walls. Joe concluded that it would take a good fire in the stove to keep his small house warm during real cold winters. No doubt this man had endured some hard times in his effort to live a simple life.

"Been over at the cemetery looking at the gravestone of Fancy Burger. I noticed that the stone doesn't have a birth date," Joe said as he sat down to get Uncle Lee's answer to the mystery.

"Fancy Burger, what a story. I reckon it was the fall of 1896 or maybe '97," Uncle Lee began.

"John, what was that?" Martha asked.

"What do you mean? What time is it?" John responded.

"There, didn't you hear that?" she asked.

"It's the wind or a cat. It can't be more than midnight. Now go back to sleep, I have a busy day coming up and I need some sleep," he explained.

"There it is again, John. I tell you there is something on our porch, and it sounds like a child crying," Martha said.

John and Martha Burger lived in one of the larger houses in Crossroads. John owned one of two barber shops in town. A large number of the men in the area came to John for haircuts and shaves. This required John to work long hours six days a week. It was work that he enjoyed because he learned the news from all parts of the community.

They were well-liked people who took part in most of the community events and played a major role in the growth of the Baptist church in town. While they had been married for twenty-five years, they did not have any children, but Martha spent a lot of her time working with the children in the community.

Just as John was about to go back to sleep, "There it is again," Martha said. "Go see what is making that noise."

"You go, Martha. If you need help call me," John encouraged.

"Well, it always seems to be my job to do things around here," Martha said as she got out of bed and put on her robe. "If it's someone intent on harming us, I guess you want me to take care of it."

"Oh, Martha I am awake now so I will go, but I tell you it will be a cat. And we don't need another cat!" John said as he got out of bed and walked to the front door. "Well of all things, would you look at this."

"Someone had left a small two or three-year-old boy on John and Martha's porch," Uncle Lee said.

"Boy! But the name on the gravestone says Fancy. That seems like a girl's name to me. I thought the grave was for a woman," Joe interrupted.

"No, Fancy was a boy, all boy," Uncle Lee said.

"Well, how did he get that name?" Joe asked.

"Martha! Come here and look at this," John called. "It's sure no cat."

"Of all things, and look isn't that the fanciest little coat you have ever seen?" Martha responded as she took the child from John.

People all over town helped them search for some information that might lead to his parents, but nothing ever turned up. Rumors were told of a young single woman at Nogo who had two children that she could not raise. But no one could ever come up with a name or person who might have left the child on the Burger porch that night. Because of the hard times no one else agreed to take the child, so he became known as Fancy Burger as John and Martha gave him a home.

It didn't take Martha long to realize that Fancy was an unusual child. By the time he was talking well enough to be understood, he was singing. Martha led singing at the Baptist church and had a good ear for music. Therefore, she quickly saw that Fancy was gifted in this area.

Since they didn't know when he was born or how old he was, they guessed him to be about two years old. He didn't have a birthday, but they always gave him gifts on the day that he was left on the porch.

By the time he was ten, he was singing specials in the Baptist church in town. People filled the church to hear him sing and share his little talk about why he loved Jesus. By the age of twelve, the pastor was letting Fancy deliver the sermons on Saturday evening. People traveled from all over to hear him preach.

Martha had nice suits made for him to wear when he sang and preached, so the name Fancy stuck with him. Before he was sixteen, he was being asked to preach Gospel meetings all over the country. Martha would travel with him to the meetings and play the piano for him.

During a Gospel meeting in Hickory on a cold November night, Fancy was preaching on Isaiah's experience in the temple. When he came to the part in his message where he repeated God's call to Isaiah asking who would go for him, Fancy stopped preaching. He stood silent for several minutes, and then he looked at the crowd and answered that he would go.

"I must be obedient to what I am asking all of you to do. I must be obedient to what God is asking of me. I must go wherever he leads me to go," Fancy said. "I sense that God wants me to become a missionary and go to places I have never heard of."

Some of the people asked those around them what missionaries were. They had never heard of those kinds of people before. Others began to pray that God would show them what they should be doing or where they should go. Before long there were women shouting and praising God. Others were testifying as to how God was speaking to them.

Night after night the revival continued for three weeks. People came from other chuches and were filled with the spirit. Young men announced their calling into the ministry. It would be remembered as the greatest revival ever to take place in that entire area.

For twenty years Fancy would do mission work in America. He started churches in a number of states across the west. But by the age of thirty-six, he sensed that God wanted him to go to other countries and preach the Gospel. In obedience to God's call, Fancy traveled to Africa and spent twenty years on the mission field.

One day in May, Crossroads received news from the mission field that Fancy had passed away while preaching the Gospel to a group of young men. John and Martha had both passed away by that time, but the town had adopted Fancy as their son. His body was returned to Crossroads for burial.

It would be the biggest event to ever take place in Crossroads. People came from all over the state. The communities where Fancy had started churches in other states sent members. Pastors who had been called into the ministry under his preaching came. The number of converts, preachers, and missionaries that had answered the call of Isaiah in his revivals was collected.

A large tent was placed in the field to the west of the cemetery for the service. The service lasted all day as speaker after speaker came forward to tell what this one man under the leadership of God had done. The show of appreciation for the work that Fancy Burger had done was unbelievable. One man simply listening to God speak through the call that Isaiah had and saying 'here am I send me' changed communities across America and Africa.

The folks in Crossroads decided to bury him at the gate to the cemetery to show the people who passed by how much they thought of him. Some began to suggest ideas for his gravestone and before long the idea of a large heart made of stone inside rings of iron symbolizing a man's heart that belonged to the world was accepted.

"I don't know, I guess the gravestone is a little odd and maybe too large, but if people had known Fancy Burger they would say it just wasn't enough," Uncle Lee said as he wiped tears from his eyes.

"You knew Fancy?" Joe asked

"Heard him preach his first sermon and his last before he left the area. Don't guess I have ever heard anyone sing like that boy could. He opened heaven's gates and the glory of God filled the building. His ability to share the Bible without any training was amazing. Preachers from all over took notes when he preached," Uncle Lee told Joe. "I don't know who dropped Fancy off on John's porch, but the boy was God-sent."

"Uncle Lee, for some reason I had never thought of you as being involved in church work. I guess it is because you are no longer able to go to church," Joe said with a look of surprise.

"Worked in the church for years until it got to where I didn't have a way to get there. The community band played for Fancy in his revivals and Gospel meetings all over the country. But when they moved the church some distance down the road, and it was too far for me to walk. I guess I got to where I just didn't think I could help much anymore," Uncle Lee suggested. "Sent my dollar by Fred ever Sunday when he came by to check on me. After he died, there wasn't anyone, so I lost contact with the church."

"I don't guess I get this Isaiah thing. I've tried church before, but it didn't ever seem to do anything for me," Joe responded trying to figure out how he could change the subject.

"Best I can remember, according to Fancy, that was what Isaiah was all about. Folks get themselves in some kind of big mess, and then they run to the church for God to take care of them. Fancy would tell about Isaiah in that kind of mess after the death of the king. Then he would stomp the floor so loud that anyone asleep in the building would jump to attention. Listen! he would cry at the top of his voice, Listen! Can't you hear God speaking to you? It's not what God can do for you. Its what can you do for God. Who will go for me? This is what he was asking Isaiah, and it is what he is asking you. Maybe that is what he wants to ask you Joe, if you will just listen," Uncle Lee explained.

"I have been thinking, I have some lumber and material left from the remodeling jobs at the house. If you will let me, I will bring them over and do some work on this room. It will make it warmer for the winter ahead," Joe offered.

"This old house is like me, it has seen its better days. But if you would like to spend a day working on it, I don't mind. That would give me time to tell you about the biggest event that ever took place in Crossroads," Uncle Lee said.

"I thought you just told me about the biggest event," Joe responded.

"No, I told you about the most important event. The hanging was a bigger one," Uncle Lee suggested.

"I'm going over to see Mattie for a few minutes. I will see if she has a day she can help me with this work on your house," Joe offered as he prepared to leave.

"Keep your ears open, Joe. God may have more for you to do than just work on an old man's house," Uncle Lee said as Joe made his way to the door and thanked Uncle Lee for the story and advice.

CHAPTER NINE

Mattie Gets Serious

"Don't move Mattie. That big red male looks like he is ready to attack," Joe screamed to Mattie as he jumped out of his car and ran to a fence post to get a hoe. "What in the world is going on here?"

"I opened their gate and turned to get the bucket of feed when they all rushed by me and into the yard," Mattie answered.

"Let me see if I can get them to back up some, and you take the bucket of feed down the fence. We will see if we can work them back to their pen," Joe said as he shared a plan with her that he thought might work. He had not participated in situations like this in New York, so he wasn't sure how he should handle this dilemma.

"They want this bucket of feed. If I move they will attack me. See that little black and white one, it is the bad one of the group," Mattie said as she watched Joe and saw that he didn't have any idea what he was doing. "You will have to drive them back toward the barn. If you can get them through that first gate we have a chance."

Joe began working to get them headed toward the gate Mattie had suggested. He would have them all moving in the right direction and then one or two would try to break off and run. After some time he had them through the gate and headed to the barn.

"Take them on to the second gate, Joe. If you can get them through that gate, close it as fast as you can. But watch out, those three red ones have had enough of you swinging the hoe at them. They may run at you any minute," Mattie explained.

"There I have them back in their pen. I didn't know farming was so dangerous. A turned ankle or skinned knee and you could be out for a day or so, then who would take care of everything around here?" Joe said.

"Well, from the way you herded those chickens back to their pen, I would say you could take care of about anything," Mattie said with a big smile on her face. "Maybe I need to consider taking on a new hand. Do you have any references that address your farming skills that I could check?"

"Now Mattie, you know I grew up in the city, but did you see how quickly I learned how to handle this very dangerous situation? I think that is just an example of what I am capable of doing around here," Joe answered. "But, I have been over at Uncle Lee's, and he told me the most amazing story about a man by the name of Fancy Burger. Have you ever heard of him?"

"I guess everyone around here has heard about Fancy. I was just a small girl when they had his funeral, but my parents took me. They wanted me to be able to say that I was at the funeral of the most important person ever to come from Crossroads. It was one of only two times I ever saw my dad cry," Mattie explained.

"From the way Uncle Lee talked, he must have been something. Do you know anything about this Isaiah and God telling people that he has work for them to do?" Joe asked.

"You not getting all religious are you? And just when I am thinking about letting you come by for visits more often. I want you to know that I don't need anyone talking that religious stuff to me, so if you are going to have any chance of a relationship with me, you will have to leave that talk off," Mattie said looking at Joe with a very serious look to show him that she meant business.

"Well, I've not had anything for religion myself since my wife and two children died, but I've never seen Uncle Lee so sure of what he was telling as he was about the message this Fancy Burger preached," Joe replied.

"I didn't know that you had been married, but I should have guessed as much. I am sorry about them dying. Can you tell me how it happened?" Mattie asked.

"I had a car wreck that killed them. I walked away without one cut, and all three of them died in the wreck. I"ve never been able to figure it out. All of the people who investigated the accident said I was the only one who should have been hurt. No one could ever explain why my wife and two children died," Joe explained as tears came to his eyes and his voice began to quiver.

"So you lost your family and you decided to move to the Ozarks and start a new life. I have never been much for running from bad situations, but maybe it has worked for you. I've had a few difficult times myself you know," Mattie said.

"And I am guessing that you are the kind of person who doesn't even believe in talking about them. Am I right about that?" Joe asked.

"They are my issues. I deal with them the best I can. People don't want you crying on their shoulders. They all have their own problems, even you," Mattie said.

"I have big shoulders. I think it would help you to talk through some of the past events in your life. That was what Uncle Lee said this Isaiah was doing at the temple when God told him he had something for him to do. I don't know, but I think we have some things in common. I think we could enjoy spending more time together," Joe suggested.

"We will spend time together if you leave the God talk off. Now I have work to do, and I am sure you have come over to watch an independent woman do the work. Besides with all that hard labor you have already done to get the chickens back into their pen, you may need the rest of the day off," Mattie said.

"Oh, that is why I came. I have some extra lumber from my projects on my house, and

I have offered to do some work on Uncle Lee's house. Could you help me tomorrow?" Joe asked.

"Tomorrow! You sure don't give a person much notice. I guess I could help after lunch. I tell you what, I will prepare a meal for all of us and meet you at Uncle Lee's about eleven," Mattie said. "Now would you like to help me clean the manure out of the barn? It will be dark in a little while."

"I guess from all I have heard about young southern people and barns, moving the manure wasn't what I thought they did in barns," Joe said.

"It's all you are going to be asked to do in this barn. Now if you will get that fork, I will show you how to use it," Mattie responded in a tone that let Joe know that for the present, only work was going to take place in her barn.

One thing was clear to Joe at this point. Mattie was willing for Joe to come by and help with the work, but as far as their relationship it only involved Joe helping with the work. Mattie was serious about that. Joe decided to change the subject and see if he could find something that Mattie would talk about that didn't create so much tension.

"You said you saw your father cry two times. What was the other time?" Joe asked.

"If that doesn't beat all, you sure can't keep your foot out of your mouth. What business is that of your's?" Mattie asked as she placed her hands on her hips to show that she meant to defend her right to keep her personal life out of their conversations.

"I don't guess I ever saw my dad cry. He left us when I was three. Mom had to work at two jobs to feed me and my sisters. We lived in a low income part of town. I had to fight boys more than once to make them leave my sisters alone," Joe said.

"Look! Let's get serious about what you are doing here. You are here to help me with this work, nothing else. I don't want a relationship with a man, and I don't intend for you or anyone else to try and force me into one. Now, are we clear about this?" Mattie asked.

Joe turned to his manure fork and continued his work in the barn. One thing was clear to Joe, Mattie must have had a bad experience with some man, and it was going to be difficult for him to change her thinking about him. But with time, he was sure he could, and he had plenty of time.

CHAPTER TEN

THE HENSON HANGING

Joe helped Mattie in the barn until dark. He discussed their plans for working at Uncle Lee's the following day with her and then got on his way to Turnbow. During the drive home he couldn't get the negative attitude she had about men off his mind. It seemed to him from what everyone had said that she loved her father even though some suggested that he was worthless.

When Joe made the turn off the highway to drive to his house, he stopped the car and backed onto the highway. He hadn't eaten at Sid's Cafe for some time, and this was a good night to correct that. Sid made the best pies he had ever tasted and this was what he wanted.

Sid did not disappoint Joe. He had a banana pie he had just taken out of the oven. Sid promised that by the time Joe completed his meal it would be cool enough to cut. In Joe's opinion this was Sid's best pie.

While Joe was eating his meal Jake made his way into the cafe. Joe had not seen Jake for several weeks, but he could see by the way he moved around that he was much better. Jake asked if he could eat with Joe since his wife was at her parents' house and would not be joining him for dinner.

As they talked over their meal, Joe learned that Jake was driving a truck and would be willing to loan it to Joe to move his material over to Uncle Lee's. He would just drive Joe's car home, and they would exchange automobiles the following evening. Jake was eager to hear about Joe's trips to Uncle Lee's. The stories Joe had heard were new to Jake, and he enjoyed a brief version of each one.

Joe happened to mention Mattie a time or two in his conversation. By the second time he called her name, Jake stopped him to ask if she had a second name. He had never heard of a person by the name of Mattie. Joe explained that her name was Mattie Haines and that she lived south of Elbow close to the man who sat on the side of the road in a rocking chair.

"Well, that explains a lot. You haven't been visiting the old man in the rocking chair, you have been visiting this Mattie Haines," Jake said raising his voice to the point that Sid overheard him.

"Mattie Haines, that name sounds familiar," Sid said as he joined in the conversation. "Who knows Mattie Haines?"

"Joe here has been out catting around on us Sid, and we thought he was working on his house and that book he keeps telling us about," Jake said.

"Wait a minute, wait just a minute. Mary, come out here if you have time," Sid called back to his wife who was working in the kitchen.

"What is it, Sid? Someone find your teeth in their meal?" Mary asked as she appeared from the kitchen.

"Joe here has been dating a Mattie Haines. Don't we know a Mattie Haines?" Sid asked.

"Let's keep everything straight here. I have not been dating Mattie Haines. I have been visiting a man who goes by the name of Uncle Lee. Mattie Haines lives down the road from his house. She needed some help this afternoon on her farm, and I helped her," Joe explained.

"Sure you did. We all understand what you mean," Jake said.

"Well, we don't talk about people's personal lives here in Turnbow, but if she is the Mattie Haines that Sid and I knew, Joe is right, he's not courting her," Mary said as everyone turned to see if she was going to tell more.

"Sounds like we have some conflict of stories here," Jake said. "Why would Joe not be courting her?"

"I have work to do in the kitchen. Sid, you need to see if the people at table three need anything to drink," Mary said as she returned to the kitchen.

Joe thanked Jake for the loan of his truck and exchanged keys with him so that he could be on his way. He needed to gather his tools and get things ready for an early start to Uncle Lee's the next day.

Puzzled by what Mary had said, Joe tried to roll over everything he had learned about Mattie Haines. It seemed to him that everything he had been told was positive. Even Mrs. Dobbins had said that she was a sweet person. It was her son who had told him to leave Mattie alone.

Uncle Lee seemed to trust her with about anything he had. She spent a lot of time helping him. That seemed like a good sign to Joe. There was something missing to the puzzle, and Joe could not come up with the pieces.

Joe didn't sleep any during the night, so he had the truck loaded and was on his way to Uncle Lee's by good light. He had a plan for improving his house, and he knew it would take some time to carry out the plan. The old house needed some work if the winter was going to be as cold as Uncle Lee had suggested. By using the material left from his house, Joe thought he could keep a lot of the cold wind out. That would give the wood stove enough help so that it would keep Uncle Lee warm during the days. He was concerned that it might be difficult for him to keep wood in the stove during the long, cold nights.

As Joe approached Elbow he looked at his watch. He had not thought about getting to Uncle Lee's too early. Joe thought he might need to stop and kill a little time before driving on over to his house. That would give Uncle Lee a little time to get up and prepare for his visit.

The only place that Joe knew of in Elbow to pull off the highway and stop was the cemetery, so he pulled over in Jake's truck and decided to wait for a while. It wasn't but a few minutes until Joe saw Mattie's car drive by on her way home. Surely she hadn't gotten up that early to go to Turnbow. But what would she have been doing out that early?

"I hope I haven't come too early," Joe said as he greeted Uncle Lee who was standing on his porch looking in the direction of the dirt road that led to Mattie's house. "Couldn't get any sleep last night for thinking about some things Mattie told me yesterday."

"Anything worth having is worth waiting for. You just have to give some women more time than others. Mattie brought me my breakfast on her way home from her night job. She said she saw you asleep in the truck over at the cemetery. She figured you thought you would wake me and decided to give me more time. I get up at four," Uncle Lee answered.

"Night job, what does she do at night around here?" Joe asked surprised that a young woman would be working at night.

"She can tell you when she is ready. Not much for any woman to do around here anymore. She will have the bank paid off in December for the money she borrowed to pay back the folks her dad owed. You will see a different person then," Uncle Lee assured Joe.

"I need to take some measurements before I get started," Joe said changing the subject.

"Come on in and I will tell you the story of the only hanging that ever took place in this county. I reckon that would have been about 1898," Uncle Lee began.

"Jess Henson was only nineteen when they hanged him at the Crossroads jail for the murders of Ed and Sara Christian. Jess claimed, up to the moment they dropped the door he was standing on, that he wasn't the one who killed the Christians, but he would not tell who did it," Uncle Lee explained.

Ed and Sara lived on a nice farm just north of Crossroads about five miles. Everyone knew that Ed had a great deal of money. He didn't mind telling people about how successful he had been. They also knew that he kept most of it in gold coins at his house. That was another point Ed was willing to openly make in public places. On different occasions Ed had loaned money to some of the people in the area that he really trusted. He would go to his hiding place and bring back a lard bucket full of coins for the person to see.

During the first week of September of 1897, Ed was in Crossroads bragging about some of the good deals he had made on his cattle and mules that he had sold. A number of people who were already jealous of Ed didn't appreciate him rubbing his success in when they had lost money on their cattle. Some of those individuals had asked Ed for loans and been turned down even though they tried to tell him that they were about to lose their farms.

There was also a group of young, lazy, worthless boys at the store when Ed paid off his summer bill. They watched him pay in gold and tell about how many more of the coins he had hidden away at home. When Ed left the store, the owner heard some of those boys talking about how easy it would be to hide in the woods near his house and watch him hide his money. They laughed at how funny it would be to have him return to his hiding place and find an empty bucket. They all seemed to agree that it would be justice for the way he took advantage of others.

Jess Henson was one of the boys in the store that day, but he wasn't with the others. He had come alone to the store to see if he could get some food on credit. He told the owner that they didn't have much to eat and his mother and sisters were hungry. The owner of the store was sorry to hear Jess's story, but the family already owed more than they would ever be able to repay.

The Henson family lived at Shady Bluff on a small hill-side farm. The father, Elbert Henson, was known as one of the meanest men in the county. He had been in jail a number of times for stealing things from neighbors and others in the area. He spent his time drinking with a group of worthless men. During those times, Elbert often bragged of going over to Ed Christian's place and robbing him.

Jess was well-liked by those who really knew him and didn't let their opinion of his father influence them. Everyone knew that Jess had been working since he was twelve at any job he could find to keep the family from starving. Jess's mother was also considered a hard worker, but his two sisters seemed to be more like their father.

Three days after Ed Christian had been in Crossroads, he along with his wife Sara were found stabbed to death in their home. A neighbor went by the house to tell Ed that his mules had broken out and were running on the road. He found Ed in the front room of the house and Sara in the kitchen. Both had been stabbed several times, and it appeared to the neighbor that Ed had put up a good fight.

When the sheriff got to the Christian home, he declared that they had been dead for two days. His conclusion was that Ed had been killed first after fighting with the person who killed him. He thought that maybe Sara had run to the kitchen to get a knife, but the killer had caught her and stabbed her before she could get anything to use to defend herself.

The neighbor who found Ed and Sara told the sheriff that he had seen Henry Smart at Ed's place about two afternoons back. He was sure that Henry had tried to borrow money from Ed a week earlier, but he thought Ed had turned him down.

Henry had a small farm that joined Ed on the west. Lightning had struck a tree and killed most of his cattle during the summer. Ed had bragged to neighbors that he had always wanted that piece of land that Henry owned, and he thought with all his bad luck, he would be able to get it by winter.

The sheriff talked with several people about the murders but learned very little. After two months it looked like the crime would never be solved. Since no one knew where Ed hid his gold, it was impossible to know whether the killer got any money or not. The sheriff had asked people to be on the lookout for anyone showing gold coins.

Over the coming weeks, a number of people were seen digging on the Christian farm. Try as the sheriff did, he could not stop them. By spring the place had been taken apart by those looking for Ed's gold.

One Friday night in June at a dance at Grapevine, a young man by the name of Bud Watson paid for a pie being auctioned with a gold coin. Bud Watson was from Shady Bluff, and it just happened that one of the individuals at the dance knew Bud and knew he didn't have that kind of money.

Bud was arrested and charged with the murders of Ed and Sara when the sheriff found two more gold coins in his shoe. Bud had been seen with Jess Henson by a number of people a few days earlier, so the sheriff arrested Jess too.

The two young men were charged with the murders and a trial date was set. The sheriff separated the two men so that they could not talk to each other. He told Bud that Jess was going to testify against him at the trial and tell that he killed the Christians and that he didn't have any part in the crime. To save his neck, Bud told the sheriff that it was Jess who killed them.

Bud explained that Jess was needing money to pay off a large debt at the store in Crossroads. Jess asked Bud to walk over to the Christians to see if he could borrow the money. He planned on telling him that he would pay it back with work over the winter. According to Bud, when Ed turned Jess down and began to make negative statements about his family, Jess became angry and pulled a knife and killed them. He knew where the bodies were in the house, something the sheriff had not made public.

At the trial Bud Watson took the stand and told everyone in the courthouse the same story. The store owner testified that Jess had paid off his debt at the store, but not with gold coins. Jess claimed that it was money he had earned working for different people in the community. Different farmers came forward and told the court that they had hired Jess to work for them and that they had paid him in money for his labor. But no matter what was said, the court relied on Bud Watson's testimony. They were both found guilty, but Jess Henson was sentenced to be hanged while Bud was given prison time.

Jess Henson was hanged until dead near the jail in Crossroads on a hot August day in 1898. People had traveled to Crossroads from all over the country to see the hanging. Tents were set up around town as the store owners and people of the community found ways to make money off of the show. It became known as the biggest event to take place in Crossroads.

"Uncle Lee, you don't seem like you believed that Jess Henson killed the Christians," Joe interrupted the story.

"Jess Henson couldn't even kill a snake. He came by here three weeks before the Christian killing wanting to know if I had some work he could do. I hired him to clean out my barn. While we were working in the barn, he ran onto a snake. I had to kill it. He said he didn't like to kill things. Before he left he asked me if I would be interested in buying his knife since he never used it. I still have it in the drawer there by the organ. He didn't even have a knife, but that didn't matter to the folks at the trial. For them, killing Jess Henson was the same as killing Elbert Henson, and everyone knew Elbert deserved it," Uncle Lee explained.

"Then who did kill the Christians?" Joe asked.

"Well now, that's another story," Uncle Lee said. "I think I hear Mattie with lunch. Maybe I can tell you the rest of the story as the two of you work on the house this afternoon."

"I see you have wasted the morning," Mattie said as she walked into the house carrying a basket of food. "I guess it will be up to me to complete this job just like it was to finish up the manure in the barn this morning. Seems like you can't find a man who will stay with a job until it is completed."

"Now Mattie, don't be too hard on Joe. Look at all the stuff he has messed up already this morning," Uncle Lee said with a chuckle.

"Have your fun. I have just about got this project figured out. Once I get started, it won't take anytime for me to finish it up. But first let's take a break and eat," Joe said.

CHAPTER ELEVEN

WHO KILLED ED AND SARA?

It took Joe three days with Mattie's help to complete his work at Uncle Lee's. He used paneling from what he had left on his house to cover the three walls that were outside walls. Those were the walls that let the wind blow through the room. The fourth wall joined the kitchen, and by closing the door most of the cold air was kept out of the living room that also served as a bedroom. The paneling was two different colors but Joe thought it blended well. He used plywood to cover the north side of the floor. That was where most of the air seemed to be coming from. And he placed clear plastic over the two windows on the north and the one on the west.

"What do you think of this northern man now, Mattie? Didn't know you had a real carpenter in the community did you?" Joe asked as he looked at his work with a sense of pride.

"That Bible you referred to the other day says that you better look out because pride goes before a fall. The way you are all swollen up over your work, you may fall any minute," Mattie said as Uncle Lee chuckled in the background.

"Well, I am willing to give you a little credit for the success of this project. Let's see, didn't you help lay that piece of plywood over there?" Joe asked.

"I am completely shocked. Now you know I don't deserve that much credit. Of course, we might ask Uncle Lee who nailed up the paneling on two of those three walls," Mattie said.

"You know I intended to do all of that, but the catch in my back the second day slowed me down some. Speaking of catch, you might want to give me your phone number just in case I get down some night about two and can't get up," Joe responded.

"Now what makes you think that I am going to drive all the way to Turnbow at two in the morning to help you up out of the floor?" Mattie asked.

"The way you been looking at me all day made me think that we were just about to the 'holding hands stage' of our relationship," Joe said. "Here is my phone number in case you should ever need me."

"Well now, it makes more sense for me to have your number. If the chickens ever make a run for it on my place again, you would be the first person I would want to call," Mattie answered.

"Sounds like something is becoming serious between the two of you. I guess it is about time. From what I saw, both of you been making eyes at each other," Uncle Lee joined in.

"I've got to turn my eyes toward home and do up the work. I am sure Joe will want to know the rest of the Henson story, and you have just about enough time to tell it before dark," Mattie said.

"I will come by and pay you for helping with my project as soon as I get this story. It would be a good night to eat banana pie over at Sid's Cafe if you have time," Joe offered.

"Eat banana pie at Sid's Cafe, now I will give that some thought," Mattie said as she made her way to the door to leave.

"She'll be free to do more in the evening now," Uncle Lee said.

"What do you mean by that? Oh, I know, Mattie will tell me when she is ready," Joe said just a little put out from being told that whatever this great mystery was, he would have to wait for Mattie to tell him. "I do have to admit that she is worth waiting for. I think she is the most beautiful woman I have ever seen."

"Before you get all worked up and rush off to her place, you need to let me finish my story about the Henson hanging," Uncle Lee said trying to turn Joe's attention back to what he thought was important at that time.

"Yeah, you said that Henson didn't kill Ed and Sara, but they hanged him anyway. Who did kill them, and was anything ever done to the real killers?" Joe asked.

At that point Uncle Lee began his version of what really happened to Ed and Sara. Joe tried to take his mind off Mattie and listen as Uncle Lee told the story.

One month after the hanging, two men dressed in white bed sheets and armed with shotguns made their way into the jail. They took the one guard that was on duty by surprise and tied him up. The two men made their way over to Bud Watson's cell and shot him. Convinced that he was dead they left the jail.

But before Bud Watson died, he told the man in the second cell that they did it. The following day sheriff Finton tried to get the prisoner to explain whether Bud meant that the two men killed Bud, or they were the ones who killed the Christians. The prisoner could only tell sheriff Finton what he heard. He didn't know what Bud meant by what he said.

Sheriff Finton started a manhunt for the two men who killed Bud Watson. He thought finding them might lead to Christian's gold and a solution to the killing. However, he was concerned that finding others who had killed Ed and Sara might prove that Jess Henson wasn't the real killer, and that would create another problem that he would have to deal with.

Uncle Lee seemed convinced that the sheriff was more interested in finding the money than the real killers. But no one really knew whether the killers even got the gold or not.

Three months passed and no one had been arrested for the murder of Bud Watson. It looked like the sheriff and the town were content to let things go. Jess Henson had been hanged and Bud Watson had been shot. Bud had testified that they had committed the crimes and now they had paid for them.

Everything had returned to normal in Crossroads even though people still talked about the hanging. Normal until Henry Smart made his way into the sheriff's office to show him three gold coins that he had found on his porch that morning.

The following morning another neighbor to Ed and Sara's place dropped by the sheriff's office to show him two gold coins that he had found on his porch. Day after day for two weeks people from around over the community came to Crossroads to report gold coins on their porches.

The sheriff was convinced that the coins didn't have anything to do with the actual killing. He decided that someone had found Ed's gold after the killing and was sharing it with people who had asked to borrow money from Ed and been turned down. Just some person getting even with Ed, he thought.

The next turn of events in the murders came when a man by the name of Leo Noland got kicked in the head by a horse. Noland only lived long enough to tell his neighbor that he had helped kill Bud Watson at the jail. He also told the neighbor that he was at the Christian house the night that they were killed. He said that he went to the barn to dig up the gold according to where Ed told him to dig. He said that the gold was not in the barn, and when he returned to the house both Ed and Sara were dead. Noland died before he could tell who killed them.

The Crossroads community was shocked when they learned of the deathbed testimony Leo Noland had given. Most of the people in the area questioned the story Noland's neighbor told about the killing. Leo Noland had been a respected member of the community for many years. He had always been an important part of the local church.

Members of the community tried to figure out who the second person would have been in the Noland story. All the people that Noland had ever been seen with were members of the local churches. He had always been a hard worker who minded his own business and spent most of his time with his family at home.

After investigating the story, the sheriff drew the conclusion that the neighbor wasn't telling the truth. While the neighbor had never been known to lie, this story just didn't fit. Some of Noland's family told the sheriff that the neighbor had attempted to borrow money from Leo a week or two before his death. They thought maybe he was just getting even with Leo for not loaning him the money. They even questioned his story about the horse kicking Leo, but nothing was ever done about that concern.

Uncle Lee stopped his story and looked at Joe. After several minutes Joe became puzzled as to whether this was all of the story or if there was more to come.

"Is that it? Did they not find the people who killed Ed and Sara?" Joe asked.

"No, they never arrested anyone for killing them. They had already hanged Jess Henson, and Bud Watson told everyone he was a part of the murders. They finally just let it go at that," Uncle Lee replied.

"What about the gold that showed up on the porches? Did they ever find out where it came from?" Joe asked.

"Yeah, Ed's neighbor that found them after the killing finally confessed to finding his gold. He made that confession on his death bed after it was too late for anyone to punish him. He said he shared the gold with all the people that Ed had turned down for loans over the years. Of course, he also admitted to keeping a good part of the gold for himself. He claimed that Ed had beaten him on several mule trades and thought he deserved it," Uncle Lee said.

"So no one ever really knew who killed Ed and Sara?" Joe said.

"I didn't say that. I said no one ever did anything about dealing with the people who killed Ed and Sara," Uncle Lee answered. "Bud Watson killed Ed and Sara."

"Bud Watson, but you said Jess Henson couldn't kill a snake," Joe said, completely confused by Uncle Lee's statement.

"Jess Henson didn't have anything to do with the killing. He met Bud Watson and two of his friends on his way over to Ed's house on the night of the murders. They talked for a while, and Jess told Bud that he was going over to Ed's to see if he could borrow some money to pay off the family debt at the store in town. Bud and his friends followed Jess over to the Christian place. They thought Ed might loan Jess the money since he was such a good boy and had worked for him at different times." Uncle Lee explained.

"They hid in the yard thinking they would watch Ed go to his hiding place and get the money for Jess. After he returned to the house, they planned on stealing the rest," Uncle Lee continued. "But Ed turned Jess down, so Bud and his friends decided to make Ed talk by threatening to kill Sara. When Ed refused to tell them where the gold was hidden, things got out of hand and they killed them."

"How is it that you know all of this and no one else seemed to know it?" Joe asked.

"His knife told me. Bud told the court that Jess Henson killed them with a knife that he had gotten in a trade from Frank and Wendell Highland. Those two boys were seen with Bud just about everywhere he went. But Jess didn't have that knife, because I had it. That was enough to let me know who killed them," Uncle Lee concluded.

"I am still confused about some of this story. How do you know that Jess Henson met Bud and his friends on his way over to the Christian place?" Joe asked.

"Jess told the people at the trial that he met them on the road and told them what he was doing. They didn't believe him after Bud told his story. When two of the people broke into the jail and shot Bud, he said they did it. He was talking about Frank and Wendell. But the sheriff couldn't talk to them because they rode their horses off into a deep hole of water and drown on their way home from the killing. I guess their shotguns fell into the deep water, and no white bed sheets were found with them. Besides they were considered Bud's good friends and not two people who would be capable of killing him," Uncle Lee explained.

"I am going to have to say this is about the best one you have told yet. There are some parts of the story that just don't seem to fit, but it sure has been interesting. Crossroads has one hanging in it's history, and they hanged an innocent person. A man is killed in the jail, and no one ever found guilty for the crime. Now how do you know the Highland boys killed Bud?" Joe asked.

"The Highland boys were considered two of the best riders in this area. They had crossed that body of water endless times.

They knew that there were only two holes of water too deep to cross on horseback. People in the area said that they heard two horses running hard by their place late that night. The only thing that would have caused them to make a mistake and ride into the deep water had to be something that really had them scared. I would say killing their best friend would have done that," Uncle Lee said with a tone and look of satisfaction that he knew what he was talking about. "You better head on over to Mattie's place. I think the two of you are working up a relationship."

Joe remembered his promise to Mattie and jumped from his chair. It was getting late, but he still had time to keep his word and take Mattie to Sid's Cafe for a meal. After all this was going to be a date.

CHAPTER TWELVE

MATTIE'S FIRST DATE

Mattie finally agreed to go with Joe to Sid's Cafe for a meal. Joe wanted to know if they could call the outing a date, to which Mattie agreed. She told Joe that she had never been on a real date before. Since this was to be her first, Joe wanted to make sure it was a good experience for her. He was hoping that it would be the first of many they might have in the future.

"Mattie Haines I haven't seen you forever," Mary said as Joe and Mattie walked over to a table to be seated at Sid's Cafe. "I guess you will be free to do more things with this fine man since Hank no longer needs your services."

"Mary, why don't you come to the kitchen and let me wait on folks for a while!" Sid called.

Joe looked at Mattie and he could see that Mary's statement had driven a knife into her heart. She had quickly changed her facial expression from one of happiness to one of fear and anger. Whoever this Hank was, Mattie didn't appreciate Mary bringing him up with Joe present.

"We want to order our meal, Mary," Joe said in a displeased tone. "And I hope Sid has a banana pie about ready to be cut. Or do you feel that our presence might cause some of the people to leave?"

"Well, of all things," Mary said as she quickly returned to the kitchen.

"I can defend myself, Joe. I guess she had some right to say what she did. Folks have their ideas about what other people are doing," Mattie said as tears came to her eyes.

"Do you want to go someplace else to eat?" Joe asked.

"No, it would probably be the same wherever we went," Mattie said.

"Don't the two of you pay any attention to Mary. Mattie it is good to see you. We were sorry to hear about Helen. She was a fine woman.

It was a hard way to go. I've got banana pie and a great special," Sid suggested.

"Sounds good to me. How about you, Mattie?" Joe asked.

"It sounds good to me," Mattie replied.

They ate their meal but noticed that others kept looking at them as if they might be out of place. Joe thought maybe it was because of him. He had received those looks from people as he walked down the street when he first came to Turnbow. He had hoped that it would change over time.

After the meal, Mattie suggested that they go back by the cemetery. Joe thought that was a strange place to park on a first date, but he didn't want to do anything else to ruin Mattie's evening.

"Uncle Lee told you the story of Fancy Burger. I want to tell you the story of one of his converts. My dad had established a reputation of being the county "everything associated with bad." When I was five, we began attending the church here in town where Fancy attended as a child. One Sunday they had ministers come to the church to tell what Fancy's preaching had done for them. When they told this Isaiah story about God calling people to go and do His work, my dad got up and told the people that he was called to preach. I can remember that my mother laughed all the way home. She never attended church again. I would go with my dad to different churches when they would invite him to speak. It wasn't long until my mother started burning his Bibles to keep him from preparing sermons. After five years of fighting with my mother, my dad gave up preaching and starting drinking again," Mattie recalled.

"Mattie, what a first date this is turning out to be for you," Joe said. "But there must be more to the story or we would not have stopped at the cemetery."

"Hank Shull grew up just over that fence in a small two- room house. He was an honest person who attended Fancy's home church. When he was eighteen he married Helen Wilson. Helen grew up over there a little closer to Crossroads. Her father ran the post office," Mattie began.

"They were six years older than me but we use to play together as children. I have known them all my life. Two years ago Helen got sick, and the doctors said she had cancer. When Hank asked me if I would help him care for her at home so that she would not have to die in the hospital, I agreed. They were my friends," Mattie continued.

"It didn't take some of the busy-bodies around here long to spread the story that Hank and I were doing things at night while his wife was dying," Mattie told Joe as she began to cry. "No matter what those folks said, I wasn't going to leave Helen. She was like a sister to me that I never had, and I guess Hank was more like a brother than a friend."

"Mattie Haines you are even a stronger person than I thought. You have been carrying some load for a long time. But I don't understand why you couldn't have shared this with me sooner. I would have understood," Joe said.

"I knew that as soon as you told people my name, you would get all of the lies that have been told about me and my father. I wanted you to decide for yourself if they were true. If I had told you my side of the story I was afraid you would have thought that I was just defending myself. I wanted my actions to defend me, not my words," Mattie said.

"So now Helen has passed away and you have lost a real friend, more like a sister," Joe said.

"She will be buried here in two days. I want you to come to the funeral with me.

But I want you to know that if we are going to be seen in public together people are going to talk. Most folks around here don't think the apple ever falls far from the tree. For you to be seen with a person like me will lead them to tell all kinds of stories on you. I just want to make sure you understand that," Mattie explained.

"And you have refused to have anything to do with me all this time because you were trying to protect my reputation. The great mystery has been your concern for what people would say about me. I don't know much about this apple falling business, but I think I have found a golden apple. One that I am willing to keep at all cost, if that is okay with you," Joe said.

As Joe drove Mattie home she noticed that the moon was full and larger than usual. The moon and cool night all caused Mattie to begin to think about what she had missed by not having a relationship with a man over the years. Of course, there just weren't that many men around Elbow she would have wanted a relationship with. Since she was a Haines, all the boys thought of only one thing when they talked to her. She always felt as though they were trying to look at her as if she was that kind of girl.

This was what she had liked about Joe from the first time she met him. He didn't have that look.

When Joe got to Mattie's home, he helped her out of the car and walked her to the front door. He thanked her for the date and was turning to leave when Mattie announced that she had never been kissed before.

"I am sure since you have been married that you have had a great deal of experience. I would only want my first kiss to come from someone with the knowledge to know how to do it right, Joe Harrison," Mattie said.

"I don't blame you, Mattie. An individual without any experience could create a bad memory for you. But I don't believe in kissing on the first date. That might lead the girl to expect too much on the second date. However, since you have your heart set on a kiss, I guess I can make an exception this one time," Joe said as he kissed Mattie good night.

As Joe drove back by Uncle Lee's place and took the highway home, he just hoped that Mattie's first date had helped her. One thing he knew, she had opened her life up to him, and he now understood why she had been acting as she had. He could live with all that she had told him, and he certainly believed what she had said. It had not been told in such a way that she was trying to defend herself. Joe was sure she was just being honest to protect him.

SUMMER OF 1906

It was a clear, warm, beautiful winter day in the Ozarks when Joe walked down his lane to the mailbox. Things had really turned around for him over the past few months. He had helped Uncle Lee improve his house for the winter. Uncle Lee had given him enough material for two books, all he needed was more time to write them.

But most of all there was Mattie, the most beautiful woman he had ever seen was now talking about a long-term relationship with him. They were calling each other regularly and spending hours talking about the future. How could life be any better in the Ozarks than he was experiencing it?

When Joe arrived at his mailbox, he came up with another reason life was so much better. Since he had his own mailbox, he did not have to make his weekly visits to the post office. That meant that he did not have to deal with Gracie Barns. He could put up with Mrs. Dobbins on his weekly visits to the grocery store, but Gracie Barns was more than he could take.

When Joe opened his mailbox door and read the note on the top of his mail, his day was ruined.

"What in the world could she want? I signed everything she said I needed to sign for the box two weeks ago. It's just another effort on her part to let me know that she is still available. I am just not going to respond to this note. I will not let it ruin my day," Joe said to himself.

"Joe Harrison please come by the post office at your earliest convenience. I have a matter I need to discuss with you, Gracie Barns," Joe read again and again as he walked back up the lane to his house.

By lunch Joe couldn't think of anything but the note Gracie Barns had sent him. He was a grown man and capable of handling people like Gracie. He decided he would go to town and have one of Sid's good lunches with a piece of banana pie. After that, he would just walk over to the post office and let Gracie know that he received his mail on a route now and did not appreciate her telling him that he needed her service at the post office. Any matters that related to mail could be dealt with by the rural carrier. That was what Joe decided to do.

After lunch at Sid's Cafe, Joe made his way over to the post office. Gracie was busy when he went in, so he waited at the back of the line. It didn't take long for the great lunch he had enjoyed at Sid's to begin to turn in his stomach as he listened to Gracie deal with some of the men standing in line.

"Well, good afternoon Joe Harrison. It certainly took you long enough to respond to my note. Do you have that kind of busy schedule?" Gracie asked as Joe walked to the window where she was working.

"It's very busy right now. I had other plans for the day, but I decided I had to deal with this matter. What did I forget to sign?" Joe asked.

"Oh, you didn't forget to sign anything. I heard you were writing a book about events that have taken place in the Ozarks, and I ran across this box of pictures. I thought they might help you with some of your stories," Gracie responded.

"This is a box of pictures of events that have taken place around here, Miss Barns?" Joe asked.

"Yes, we collected them here for years, but now that everyone has a camera, people make their own pictures. I thought I would loan them to you, and you can go through them to see if they will be helpful. You can return them when you are through with them. I think you will find the notes written on the back of each picture will give you information about the time and place of the event being recorded," Gracie said.

Joe thanked Gracie for all the help. He promised to return all the pictures as soon as he could and that he would take good care of them in the meantime. Joe made his way back to his car and quickly drove home. This is what he had been looking for. Some visual proof of the stories Uncle Lee had told him.

Sorry that he had developed such a negative attitude toward Gracie Barns, Joe made his way to the kitchen table. Excited about what the pictures might reveal about the area, he opened the box and began to place the pictures on the table. Just as Gracie had said, each picture had names, places, and dates on the backs. This was more than Joe could have ever hoped for. It was a pictorial record of events that must have been important to the people of the area.

Joe began to organize the pictures according to dates and areas. He was especially interested in those from Crossroads (Elbow). It took Joe the rest of the afternoon to sort all of the pictures, but by the time he was through, he had a good, large stack of Crossroads pictures. In an effort to take a break after hours of work, Joe called Mattie to share his excitement.

After a long break and visit by phone with Mattie who shared Joe's excitement about what he had found, Joe returned to his work. He divided the pictures from Crossroads by dates and began to look for some of the things that Uncle Lee had told in his stories. There were a numbers of pictures of the town from different times.

The oldest picture that Joe could find was the hanging of Jess Henson. It was just like Uncle Lee had said. The town was full of people for the hanging and all seemed to want their picture made.

Stella's boarding house was in several pictures. Uncle Lee must have been correct about that event. It must have really been a big deal for the people in Crossroads.

There were several pictures of the school. The boys' basketball team that won the state championship had a number of pictures. That was a big event for the town. Some of these pictures created questions for Joe. He quickly found some paper and a pencil and began to write down questions that he could ask Uncle Lee on his next visit.

It was at that point that three pictures really caught Joe's attention. All three pictures were of men holding up large rattlesnakes. The date on the pictures was 1906 and the information stated that the snakes were killed during the rattlesnake migration of '06. Joe didn't know anything about snakes, but he had never heard of a snake migration. This was certainly something that he needed to discuss with Uncle Lee. If the town had saved three pictures of the same event, it must have been a big deal.

Joe had planned on visiting Mattie in a couple of days. He intended to stop by and see how Uncle Lee was doing. But this was too big of an issue for Joe to wait, he needed to learn more about this rattlesnake migration as soon as possible.

Early the following morning after a sleepless night, Joe drove to Elbow to see Uncle Lee, and, of course, Mattie. It was after eight when Joe knocked on Uncle Lee's door, but he found him still in bed.

"Thought you said you were always up by four. My watch must be wrong," Joe said as he walked into the room.

"Not been feeling well the last day or two. I didn't get much sleep last night. Guess I ought to get up and fix some breakfast," he responded. "You had anything to eat?"

"I ate some time ago. Let me fix you something. I am about as good with eggs and bacon as you'll find," Joe offered.

Joe moved to the kitchen and began looking for the things he would need to cook breakfast for Uncle Lee. As he prepared his meal, Joe told Uncle Lee about the pictures Gracie Barns had loaned him. Joe explained how the pictures matched up with his stories. Of course, Uncle Lee had to ask if that meant that Joe had been doubting them.

"I can't say that I doubted them, but some of them sure stretched my thinking," Joe answered trying to be as honest with Uncle Lee as he could.

"I guess when a person from the state of New York runs into a rich history like this town has, it is hard for him to believe everything he is told. And, of course, it has been some time since a lot of this happened. I have to admit I might not have all my facts straight," Uncle Lee explained.

"I found three pictures from 1906. All three pictures were of men holding up large rattlesnakes. Do you know anything about the picture called the rattlesnake migration?" Joe asked.

After Uncle Lee ate his breakfast he sat down in his rocker and began the story behind the 1906 pictures. As he looked at the three pictures, he thought the second one was of him and two of the men who lived down the road from his place at that time. He wasn't sure because his eye sight was fading. He told Joe that the other two men had passed away several years back.

"In 1905 there was talk all over the area of a railroad coming up the valley just east of Crossroads. At that time railroads were being built back into the mountains. Companies wanted the good oak timber that existed in the mountains. They also needed a better way of getting the cotton out of the area," Uncle Lee explained. "All of the towns wanted a railroad because it made growth possible. The towns that were missed by the railroads were afraid that it would hurt their growth."

"I guess that proved to be true. But I haven't seen any railroads anywhere in this area. What happened to them?" Joe asked.

"When the rich folks got all the timber, they didn't need the rail lines anymore, so they stopped running trains into the mountains. The world war also hurt the area and the depression really did a lot to stop the trains from making any money in the area," Uncle Lee said.

"But what did a railroad have to do with this rattlesnake migration?" Joe asked concerned that he was going to get another one of Uncle Lee's stories that might not be completely correct.

By 1906 the route for the railroad had been established, and it was going east of Crossroads. The long valley to the east made it possible for the company known as the Ozark Mountain Line to build the track at a very fast pace with little cost. The only problem, according to Uncle Lee, was the mountain just north of the town.

For years people had talked about all the rattlesnake dens in the rocks along the top edge of the mountain, but they had never bothered anyone in the valley. The folks who lived around the mountain just stayed away from the cliffs during the summer.

In the summer of '06, the railroad workers began using black powder to blast out the hillside so they could continue the line on over to Pleasant Valley and Rageville. Uncle Lee was convinced that the blasting was what started it all.

Josh Washburn and his oldest son Jacob were killing some meat for the table early one morning when their dogs treed a rattlesnake. After they had killed the snake, they began to look around and discovered that they were standing in the middle of several snakes. They caught their dogs and made a run for the house.

"You get the milk cows out of the pasture and bring the mules in, Jacob," Josh told his son. "I will saddle the horse and ride down the valley to warn the people that the snakes are coming. It must be the blasting on the cliffs. I have never seen rattlesnakes migrate like this before."

Josh stopped at all the farm houses down the valley as far as Crossroads to tell the people what he had seen. He found it very difficult to get most of them to believe him even though he was considered an honest man. Those people who did believe Josh began to think of ways they could protect their animals and families from the snakes.

Before long, shots could be heard all along the valley. People were killing snakes as fast as they could when they came around their homes. But no matter how many they killed, the snakes just kept moving down the valley from the cliffs on the mountains.

Cattle, hogs, mules, horses, and dogs were no match for all the snakes. Many of the farmers reported livestock being bitten by enough snakes that they were killed. Even after the snakes passed, some families slept in their wagons with fires burning around, afraid they would return. Most reported that there were so many that they could not keep them out of their houses and barns.

By the time the snakes reached Crossroads, men and women had formed a line around the north and east sides of town. People had guns, shovels, axes, pitchforks, and clubs ready in an attempt to keep them out of the town. The plan was to kill as many as they could and drive the rest back toward the mountain to the west.

"Whatever you do folks, don't let any get by you," the sheriff encouraged. "We have to make our stand here, or we may lose our town to them."

"Riders have been sent out to the south of town to ask the farmers from that area to come and help," Red Smith told the people.

"When they get here, we will form a line on the the west and try and stop all the snakes right here," the sheriff responded.

"Sheriff, what will we do if the snakes do not get here until dark? We won't be able to see them at night." someone asked.

"I have people bringing in oil for lamps, and we will have people bringing up wood so that we can start a fire to keep them back at night if there are that many," the sheriff replied.

"I see one coming now," someone called out.

"That's a dead stick," another said. "Are we going to start killing dead sticks?"

After watching for the snakes for two days, a cry came from one of the men, "That's not a dead stick over there. Here they come," the guard called out.

With that warning, the killing began. The folks along the line to the north and east killed snakes off and on all day. By evening of the third day it looked like the migration was over. Men had laid wood around the line, and a fire had been started each evening. People took turns of sleeping and guarding the town. They made sure the fire did not burn down anywhere along the line at night.

By morning of the fourth day, some of the men volunteered to walk along the grounds to the north of the line and see if any more snakes could be found. When they returned and reported that they had not found any, all the people rejoiced.

Several pictures were made of the piles of snakes that had been killed. Later farmers from around the area brought their wagons to town and loaded up the snakes with pitchforks to feed to their hogs.

"Had it not been for the pictures of wagon loads of snakes, folks would never have believed that such a thing could have happened," Uncle Lee concluded.

"But Uncle Lee, the three pictures do not show wagon loads of snakes. They only show three men in each picture holding up two snakes each," Joe said.

"Is that a suggestion that you are having a hard time believing my story?" Uncle Lee asked.

"Well, I guess I could look through the rest of the box of pictures. Maybe I will find some with those wagons of snakes you mentioned," Joe suggested.

---------CHAPTER FOURTEEN---------

THE ANVIL GAMES

Joe drove over to Mattie's house thinking about Uncle Lee's story of the snakes. He was also thinking about what he had observed in Uncle Lee's ability to move around the house and eat. He had talked with Mattie different times about how Uncle Lee was declining in health. He had tried to discuss with Mattie a plan for him when he got to the point that he wasn't able to stay by himself. Mattie had her head set that she would care for him, and Uncle Lee would stay home. Joe wasn't sure that plan would work out.

"Well, now isn't that just like a man. He always shows up at meal time. I guess you expect this meal to be free just like all the others you have enjoyed at my table?" Mattie said.

"I would be willing to pay for the meal, but I am going to guess that this meal will cost me more in the long run than any meal I could get at Sid's," Joe answered.

"Since I have more to do today than I can get done and wasn't planning on cooking, why don't you just go back over to Sid's?" Mattie asked.

"I'm not really hungry, but I do have some serious business about Uncle Lee to discuss with you. Maybe I could just follow along behind you and talk while you work. I am learning so much about farming by watching you," Joe said with a tone that suggested he might be kidding.

"If you are going to talk about Uncle Lee's health, I already know how he is doing. I was over there early this morning and he didn't want to get up. I know what that means without you telling me," Mattie said.

"I think it's his mind too. He told me the most unbelievable story about a rattlesnake attack," Joe started to tell.

"That was the rattlesnake migration of the early 1900's," Mattie interrupted. "I think I still have a picture somewhere in the house of Uncle Lee standing by a wagon with a pitchfork loading dead snakes. I will see if I can find it some day when I don't have all this work to do."

Joe was speechless. He looked at Mattie to see if he could tell whether she was telling the truth or just about to break into a rolling laugh. As far as he could tell she seemed serious. But how could such a story have been true?

"Mattie, we must talk about his health. I think we need a workable plan for caring for him. And I think we will have to put that plan into action very soon," Joe said.

"I have a plan and it will not change. Uncle Lee is the only grandfather I have ever known. I don't even know who my real grandparents were. I never did see them," Mattie told Joe. "When I was young we lived in the house across the field from his house. It was his father's old house. Up unto the age of five when I heard my daddy coming home drunk, I would hide under the bed and hope that my mother and father would not fight.

By the age of five, I learned to run out the back door and through the field to Uncle Lee's house. I would spend the night with him, and he would tell me stories to keep me from being afraid. He would pick me up and set me on his lap and put pennies on the table to teach me to learn to count. After I learned to count, he used a pencil and paper to teach me my ABC's. I learned to read sitting in his lap at the table. He always had candy to reward me when I did a good job. He almost taught me to play the fiddle, but I just never could get it. Now Joe for the last time, I have a plan for him when he gets to the point he cannot care for himself, and you nor hell itself will change that plan. I hope I have made myself clear about this."

"Mattie, I think you have a good plan. I just hope that you will let me help you carry it out. I guess I didn't know he meant that much to you. I can see I have been trying to run your business when it wasn't any of mine. Now you probably don't have a banana pie, but potatoes, ham, beans, and cornbread will be fine with me. Do you need any help in the kitchen?" Joe asked.

"Come on to the house. I can see I am not going to be able to run you off. Just an old stray dog that I made the mistake of giving some food, and now I have you to take care of. While I cook I have some pictures that you might want to look at. Some of them are of events that took place in Crossroads," Mattie told Joe.

Joe looked through the pictures that Mattie shared with him. Several of them were copies of the pictures that Gracie Barns had loaned him from the post office. One picture stood out. It was a man holding an anvil in each hand. There were others in the background and several bales of cotton. The name on the back was Mahan, but it did not have a first name or date. Joe took a few minutes to look at the picture and decided that he would show it to Uncle Lee. He was sure there might be a story in this man by the name of Mahan.

After lunch, knowing that Mattie had a lot to do around the barn, Joe thanked her for the wonderful meal. He tried to offer to help Mattie for the afternoon but was quickly rejected. With nothing for him to do on the farm, he made his way back over to Uncle Lee's. He wanted to know about the picture, and he wanted to see how Uncle Lee was doing.

"Mattie shared a rather strange picture with me. Do you know anything about this Mahan and the anvils he has in his hands?"

Joe asked as he handed the picture to Uncle Lee.

"Oh, I remember the Mahans and the reason for that picture. The Mahans lived on the Persimmon Pond. There were about four of the boys. They were honest, hardworking boys. This one was about as strong as any man I ever saw," Uncle Lee told Joe as he handed the picture back to him.

"What was he doing in this picture? Was he showing everyone how strong he was?" Joe asked trying to get Uncle Lee into the story behind the picture.

"I reckon that picture was made in the '20's. Back then everyone had some kind of a cotton patch. People all around here picked the cotton in the fall, and the men brought it to Crossroads to the gin. There would be wagons backed up all over the gin yard. Sometimes these men would have to wait all night to get their cotton ginned off their wagons so that they could return home to get another load," Uncle Lee explained. "To kill time, these fellows created games for sport. The main game in the beginning was horse shoes, but after a while other games were created."

"Is that what this picture is all about? Is this Mahan playing some kind of game at the cotton gin?" Joe interrupted to ask.

"He is showing that he was the winner of the anvil games. Every year at the end of the ginning season a winner was to be declared and his picture was to be made. I guess that was before the big blow up that ended the games after the first year," Uncle Lee said.

With that introduction from Uncle Lee, the story of the anvil games began. According to Uncle Lee Jess Mahan, the man in the picture, purchased an anvil from Mr. James who was the owner of the blacksmith shop on the west side of town. He decided to carry it back across town to the gin yard instead of taking his wagon down to pick it up. While carrying the anvil he met the Cliffton brothers at the local grocery store. Intent on seeing how long they could talk to Jess Mahan before he had to put the anvil down, they talked for one hour with Mahan finally telling them that his wagon was empty, and he had to get back home to get another load of cotton.

The Cliffton family was made up of ole man Cliffton, his wife, and three boys; Orville, Clide, and Junior. The family lived in Old Piney Ridges south of Mortonville. They were the only family that lived in that area, and since it was some distance to a school, none of the boys ever attended school on any kind of regular basis.

The boys made their money trapping animals for fur in the winter time and making moonshine. They raised some cotton during the year but were too lazy to work the field, and often failed to pick much of it during harvest season. The entire family was known for their lack of interest in work. Most crimes of missing food, animals, clothing, and tools in the area were accredited to them. But for some reason the sheriff never seemed to be able to prove anything.

The boys were known more for their smell during trapping season than anything else. When they came to Crossroads, people would try to avoid the stores they shopped in because of the smell of skunk that followed them everywhere they went. The store owners hated to see them coming and tried to do business with them as fast as possible to get rid of them.

The boys took great pride in letting the people they talked to know how successful they were at trapping animals. This was something they didn't have to tell because they always had hides on their wagon, often considered by most to be stolen.

The second thing they took great pride in was their ability to whip anyone who

got in their way. They considered themselves to be the strongest men in the area.
This was a brag that had been challenged
by some who suggested that the Mahans
were the strongest men they had ever
seen. The fact that people disagreed with
them caused them to discuss how they
could prove that they were stronger than
the Mahans and be sure they won.

They had tried at different times to pro-
voke the Mahans into fighting them, but
the Mahans had always refused. Instead of
making them look like they were afraid,
however, the people witnessing the effort
always took the Mahans' side suggesting
that they were the winners for not taking
their dares.

Having met Jess Mahan on the street that
day carrying the anvil, gave Clide an idea.
The idea was one that Orville and Junior
weren't too pleased with. Clide insisted that
they could go up to the gin yard and chal-
lenge the men there to an anvil carrying
contest. The person who carried the anvil
by the horn the greatest distance would be
the winner. Orville tried to tell Clide that
Mahan had carried an anvil all the way
across town, but Clide had the idea, and he
wouldn't let go of it.

When they arrived at the gin yard, the Mahans were gone, but the people were talking about what they had seen Jess Mahan do with the anvil. Clide quickly suggested than Orville could carry the anvil across town, and he could carry it by the horn. He didn't tell the group who had gathered around Jack Smiley's wagon that they had talked to Jess Mahan for almost an hour with him holding the anvil. With his offer of what Orville could do, the bet was on. It just happened that they could not find another anvil in town that was available for them to use. But the idea had been offered and the games had begun.

Within two days an anvil had been loaned to the gin yard for the contest. The contest had been expanded to not only carrying the anvil by the horn but also throwing it. The rules had been set that the winner would have to carry the anvil by the horn the greatest distance and also throw it the greatest distance to be the winner. People would be able to compete throughout the ginning season with the winner being declared after the last bale of cotton was ginned.

Orville, not sure he would be able to win the contest with just the two events, suggested a third event. He considered himself the best with black powder of any man anywhere. He offered the idea that a third part of the contest would be shooting the anvil. The person would have to load the anvil with black powder and shoot it the highest off the ground to win. The man with the best overall record of the three events would be declared the winner.

As men came to gin their cotton, they took turns trying to improve their records in two of the events. The records were kept on a large board for all to see how they were doing and who had the lead. Because of the noise that shooting anvils made, the gin owner had refused to let them hold that event until the last day of the contest. This meant that the winner would not really be known until the last day. It also meant that everyone in the running for the champion-ship would have to be present on the last day.

It looked like the Cliffton brothers had come upon a good idea. More people made their way to Crossroads, and this made the store owners happy. Excitement was build-ing in the area, and people were talking about making this a regular yearly event.

Jack Smiley had the most cotton to pick and the least help, so he always had the last bale to be ginned each year. People watched him to see when he would be through picking so that they could predict the day for the last events.

The day finally came when Jack brought his last bale of cotton to the gin. People had gathered from all over the area to watch the anvil shoot and see who the winner would be. At that point in the contest, Jess Mahan had a long lead in the carrying event. The throwing event was almost a tie between Jess and Orville. The anvil shoot would no doubt produce the winner.

Orville had asked that he be last in the shooting event because he was sure he would be the winner. To his surprise, all of the Mahans had done much better than he had expected. Jess Mahan's shot had gone higher than Orville had ever been able to shoot an anvil. This caused him to load the anvil with more black powder than he had ever used. Clide and Junior cautioned Orville to take some of the powder out, but he refused. Sure of what he was doing, he set off his charge. The charge was so powerful that it blew out the side of the anvil and hit both Orville and Clide.

After the doctors, who were present to watch the event, cleaned Orville and Clide's wounds, they dressed the wounds telling Orville that they did not think that he would ever walk again. They were not sure about Clide, but thought that he should have his right arm removed, something he refused to do until he talked to his father. Later in the day they were loaded onto a wagon, and some of the men took them home.

People tried to celebrate the contest. Jess Mahan was declared the rightful winner, and his picture was made holding the two anvils. But the accident had created an air of concern about the possibility of holding it again. There was also a concern about what ole man Cliffton would do when he saw his two boys. He had a reputation for having a high temper and doing things to get even when he didn't get his way.

Some of the folks in town had even asked the sheriff to take Orville and Clide home just to make sure the old man was told the truth of what had happened. This was a suggestion the sheriff should have taken, but he was busy with other responsibilies and passed that job on to some of the men in town.

Junior rode his mule on ahead of the wagon to tell his folks what had happened in Crossroads. He told his dad that the

Mahans had challenged the Clifftons to the contest, and the people in town had backed the Mahans in the contest making it such a big deal that Orville and Clide had to win to defend the Cliffton name. By the time the wagon arrived, ole man Cliffton was so hot that he was declaring war on the town and especially the Mahans.

Two weeks after the tragic event in Crossroads, on a cold, wet, windy night the cotton gin burned. Most of the cotton had already been moved to the railroad loading area, but it was a major loss to the town. The sheriff investigated the fire but couldn't find any evidence to tie it to the Clifftons. Afterall, Orville couldn't walk because of the accident. Ole man Cliffton and Junior had taken Clide to Turnbow to have his arm removed because of infection that had set up in the arm. The sheriff didn't think that Mrs. Cliffton would be capable of such crime, so no one was ever charged.

A week after the fire in Crossroads, Josh Mahan, the youngest Mahan, was killing some table meat in the Persimmon Pond Ridges when someone fired on him. The shot hit his hat, but it didn't hurt him. He could only see the back of the person who fired the shot, but he returned fire causing the person to run. He wasn't sure he had hit the person, but in his mind he was sure that it had to be a Cliffton.

When the sheriff went to talk to the Clifftons about the shooting, he was informed that Junior had been kicked in the head by his mule and killed. They had buried him in the family cemetery and were now planning on moving to Mortonville. Orville and Clide were no longer able to trap animals for their fur, and they would not be able to live on the cotton Mrs. Cliffton could plant and pick. They were going to have to support themselves in some other way at Mortonville. The sheriff knew that this meant selling moonshine or stealing, but that would be the sheriff's problem in Mortonville, so he let it go.

"Did the people in the area think that it was Junior Cliffton who shot at Josh Mahan, and Josh's shot killed Junior?" Joe asked.

"I don't know about that. I am sure some may have thought that, but the way Junior beat on that old mule I would not doubt but what it just kicked him to get even," Uncle Lee answered with a smile.

CHAPTER FIFTEEN

JACK PAYNE'S WEDDING

It had been over a week since Joe had made a visit to Uncle Lee's or Mattie's. He had talked with Mattie a number of times each day, but his work on the book he was writing had kept him busy. Uncle Lee had given him so many stories that he was having a difficult time putting them into form in the book.

"I cannot believe this," Joe said to himself as he looked out his living room window. "I left upper-state New York to get away from a mother-in-law and the bad winters and look at this. It is snowing in the Ozarks before Christmas. And I had promised Mattie that

I would eat the Christmas meal with her and Uncle Lee."

Joe returned to his typewriter to read the last page of the story he had written the night before. His reading was interrupted by the phone. He knew it had to be Mattie because she was the only person who knew his number.

"I guess she is going to ask me again to marry her," Joe said to himself as he walked to the phone.

"Hello Mattie, calling to tell me that you have changed your mind about marriage?" Joe asked as he answered the phone.

"No, I don't think I would be interested in marrying a person by the name of Joe Harrison. Besides, I have a wife and four children that take about all of my time," the voice on the phone answered.

"Well, I guess I thought you were someone else," Joe said, fighting for something to say that might explain his first statement.

"I am Joseph Clark, Mr. Harrison. I work at the hospital in Clinton. Mattie Haines brought Mr. Lee in this morning, and she asked me to call you. He is in pretty bad shape, and she is in the room with him," Joseph explained.

"Tell Mattie I will be there as soon as I can," Joe replied.

This meant Mattie needed help with Uncle Lee. Joe changed his clothing as quickly as possible and made his way to his car. It was snowing, but Joe had driven on snow most of his life. Since it didn't snow that much in Turnbow, Joe did not think there would be other drivers on the road to slow him down.

By the time Joe made it to the hospital, the doctor had already made his visit to talk with Mattie. As Joe had expected, the news wasn't that good. Uncle Lee's age and several problems made it impossible for the doctor to offer much hope of a recovery.

Joe had never faced a situation like this before. He didn't have any idea what a person should say. He knew what Uncle Lee meant to Mattie; she had told him enough times. Joe had also become attached to him. He enjoyed his stories and sense of humor. But he was more than that to Joe. There was something about him that let you know that he was the real deal. He was a man that told it like he saw it, but didn't mind if you disagreed with him. He was from another generation and time, and there were few left like him. That was what Joe had tried to capture in the way he told Uncle Lee's stories in his book.

Mattie met Joe outside Uncle Lee's room. She explained to Joe that he wasn't to suggest in anything that he said that he felt sorry for Uncle Lee. She wanted him to act like everything was the same as if he were back at his house on a daily visit to get information for a story.

"Well, I see you didn't care much for the remodeling Mattie and I did for you," Joe said as he walked into the room. "Let the first snow fall, and you make a run for the hospital. Surely you didn't think our work would fall in on you?"

"Been having a little trouble eating," Uncle Lee responded. "I think it may have been from all the dust you stirred up driving all those nails in the walls. I'll be okay in a day or two. No use going back home in the snow."

"While you are in such a fine place and can get more rest than usual I would like to ask for your help with a problem Mattie has presented me with. She keeps trying to get me to make a proposal for marriage, and I don't know if now is the right time to do that," Joe explained.

"Yeah, Mattie has been telling me for the past three weeks that every time you talk to her you ask her to marry you," Uncle Lee answered. "She seems to have the same problem you have. She isn't sure that she is ready for marriage. Reminds me of the Jack Payne wedding. I guess it was the biggest wedding in these parts."

Uncle Lee laid back in his bed and closed his eyes. Jack Payne was an old bachelor who lived on some of the best farm land in the Crossroads area. His grandparents had been some of the first people to move to the area. They had farmed the land and passed it down to their sons. By Jack's generation he was the only member of the family and inherited everything. This made him a wealthy man for that time.

Jack had continued to live on the old home place but had never been interested in finding a wife. He was content to live alone and train pointer bird dogs. By the '40's, Crossroads was known for some of the best quail hunting anywhere in the state. Doctors and lawyers from Little Rock and other areas came to Jack's place to camp and hunt each year.

The quail hunting season had grown into a rather large event by the early '40's. The men who came to Jack's farm to hunt employed women from the area to do their cooking and cleaning. The women bought all their supplies from the stores in Crossroads. With different groups coming in to hunt over a two-month period, the amount the women spent in town added up. The hunters always made a number of trips into Crossroads for things they needed. They even attended the basketball games and other events in town, especially those events around Christmas.

The one common question that all groups of hunters seemed to ask was why Jack Payne wasn't married. It was about the third year of the 1940's that some of the hunters came up with an idea about how to fix what they saw as Jack's problem.

"Fellows, I think we need to find Jack a mate. He has all this land and a big house. He needs someone to help him train his dogs," one of the hunters said to the group.

"I've got an idea. I saw some women in a mail-order catalog the other day. They are all looking for a man to marry. We will be able to fix old Jack up real good with one of them," another suggested.

"Jack doesn't need a mail-order bride. He needs a real young looker. One who can spend his money in a year or two on trips around over the country and things like that," a third hunter joined in.

"No, I am serious. We need to find Jack a nice, good-looking woman about his age. One who would be at home out here on the farm," the first hunter said in an effort to let the group know he was thinking of someone who would really make Jack a good wife.

"If you are serious about this wife for Jack, how do you think we will be able to find a middle-aged woman who isn't already married? A woman who would be willing to move out here to the back side of nowhere and live a lonely life with a man who cares more about pointers than he would her?" one of the fellows asked.

"I still say the mail-order catalog is the only way to go. Those women are so desperate they would be willing to live with Jack's dogs just to get a man," the hunter added.

"I know a perfect woman. She cleans house for us three days a week. I don't think we will find a better match," Sam joined in.

"Hell, Sam that woman is black. Now do you think Jack Payne or even the community of Crossroads will accept a black woman?" another hunter replied.

"Yeah, I guess that would be overdoing it a little. But if the woman has to be a white woman we are going to have a real problem solving this matter," Sam responded.

"I can tell you why Jack isn't married. I think you fellows may be starting something that might just cause Jack to tell us we aren't welcome around here anymore. That would mean that you will lose the best quail hunting land you have ever seen. You need to think about that," one of the doctors who hunted on Jack's place every year said.

"Okay, tell us why Jack isn't married. That might help us in finding him a wife," Sam said.

"Seems like he fell in love with a young woman from over around Timberline, according to what I was told by the blacksmith. They made plans to get married, and Jack invited a lot of people to the wedding. When the day of the wedding came, the young woman didn't show up. With all the people in town talking about how Jack had been stood up, he retreated to his farm and has lived his life here alone," the doctor said.

"Oh, my, there is nothing worse than being stood up at the church. I had a brother who got stood up. He found the man that his bride ran off with and beat him nearly to death. He never did marry after that," someone added.

"Yeah, fellows I think we need to be careful here in how we handle this. We don't want to lose our hunting rights just because we are trying to do a good deed," Sam concluded.

The search was on for the right woman for Jack Payne. They also needed a way to match them up without Jack thinking that they were trying to run his life. By the last month of quail season, Sam had come up with the perfect woman. She wasn't that young, and she wasn't that good looking, but there was something about her that let Sam know she was the one.

Sam rushed Molly Sue over to the meeting he had called so that the other fellows could see her. Molly Sue had never been married, but she was looking for just the right man (any man) and Sam assured her he knew who that man was. The fact that she would be living on an isolated farm among ten to twenty pointers didn't scare her. So Sam was convinced he had the woman of Jack's dreams. At least he knew she would fit somewhere in his dreams.

"Sam have you gone mad? That is without doubt the most homely looking woman

I have ever seen." Sam's neighbor said as he pulled Sam off to one side. "How in the world do you think you could ever talk Jack Payne into marrying her?"

The group met in a back room to discuss Sam's idea of a bride for Jack. Not one single person agreed with Sam. And no one could come up with any idea as to how they could get the two together.

"We'll just take her out to camp with us next week and let her work her own way into Jack's heart," Sam suggested. With no other ideas being offered, that was accepted as the solution.

On Monday the men packed their hunting gear and along with Molly Sue made their way to Crossroads and Jack Payne's place to spend the rest of the hunting season. For the first week Molly did everything she could think of to get Jack's attention. Everything she tried failed, and by the end of the week she was rather disappointed. Different men in the hunting party joined in with suggestions of things that might work. Molly quickly tried all of those suggestions with no success.

Nothing seemed to be working until the hunters came in for lunch one day. Jack wanted to show them a young dog he was having trouble training. He really liked the dog, but didn't think he was going to be able to break him. Jack showed them the dog and tried to get him to point a dead bird, but without any success. It was at that point that everything changed.

"That method won't work with that pup," Molly Sue said as she walked over to Jack.

"And I guess you have been training pointers for thirty years and know about all there is to know, do you?" Jack asked as he looked at Molly Sue.

"Worked with my dad long enough to know that you will never train that pup to hunt with the methods you are using," she replied.

"Well now, there is nothing more than I would enjoy than to have a woman show me up in front of all the hunters. Why don't you just give us a lesson on how this should be done," Jack said as he handed Molly Sue the rope he had on the pup.

Within fifteen minutes Molly had the pup pointing the dead quail and retrieving it to her hand. When she turned the pup loose, he made a run and then turned and came in to hunt with her in the field south of Jack's house. After several minutes of letting the pup run, she called him in and put him back on the rope to give to Jack.

"Saw the pup in the pen behind the house this morning while you were hunting. I could tell he was special, so I worked him some on one of the chickens from your pen. He looks to me like he could be about the best dog you will have to hunt next year," Molly suggested.

All the hunters began to back up and talk about things they needed to do. They didn't know how Jack Payne would respond to being outdone by a woman, and they didn't want to stay around and see. To their surprise, it was love at first sight for Jack. Any woman that knew how to break a pointer pup was the woman he had been looking for.

The give and take for the rest of the week between Jack and Molly suggested that this would be a relationship where the two would never agree on anything. But that was just what both of them seemed to want. Sam admitted to the other hunters that he had never seen two happier people when they were arguing over training dogs, farming, and everything else.

As the town folks learned of the new love affair, they began to make plans for a wedding. All the people agreed that this could not be just the average wedding. This wedding had to be the biggest wedding ever in the community.

In the meantime Jack was making his own plans for the wedding. Molly and Jack agreed that the wedding would be at his house, and everyone would be invited to attend the event. Jack would get married in his best hunting clothes and Molly in her best dress.

It was at that point in the planning that an interesting question was raised. Did Jack ask Molly to marry him or did Molly someway just suggest that they should get married? Or did the folks in town start planning a wedding that they just thought was about to take place? For three days the two of them debated this question until Sam finally offered a solution. It was a solution that no one ever learned. Whatever it was, it worked and the wedding was back on.

The community band agreed to do the music for the wedding. All the members knew Jack. This was a big event, so they came up with a number of songs to play that they thought would be fitting. They also added in one or two that some of the members made up, just for Jack.

Rev. Milford Long was asked to do the wedding. Rev. Long had a long-standing reputation of marrying folks in the community who didn't believe in making religion a part of their lives. He was also known for adding a little humor to his weddings. While the ladies of the School Improvement Society didn't approve of Rev. Long, he was just what Sam and the boys thought Jack and Molly's wedding needed.

The ladies of the School Improvement Society had agreed to do the food and drinks. Clara and Sara had made a washtub of lemonade. They placed four dippers around the sides of the tub so that people could serve themselves. Other members of the society had made different kinds of eats for the wedding.

Yes, Sam and the boys managed to add a little spice to the lemonade after the activities got underway. It didn't take long for most of the men to discover what had happened, and they were lined up at the washtub waiting for a dipper.

"Clara, this lemonade has an interesting taste." one of the members of the society said. "Did you put a little sassafras in it to give it that biting taste?"

"No, Clara and I didn't put any sassafras in our lemonade. If you will look at the line waiting for more, you will see that we do a very good job making lemonade," Sara told the members who had joined them.

"Well, I will say the men sure do seem to be enjoying it," one of the members added.

By the time the community band had finished their songs that they wanted to play, all the men were in good spirits and ready for old Jack and Molly to marry. Sam encouraged Rev. Long to settle everyone down and proceed with the ceremony. Rev. Long attempted to do as Sam had requested, but since he had enjoyed several cups of lemonade, he found it difficult to find the words to get the wedding moving forward.

It was at that point that an old red rooster flew over the chicken pen fence and into the yard next to the dog pens. This rooster had been in the habit of doing this before, so the dogs were ready. Twenty pointers began barking and trying to get out of their pens so that they could catch that old red rooster. With the music of twenty barking pointers in the background, Jack and Molly said their 'I do's", and the wedding was declared a big success by Sam and the boys.

Without question it was the most unusual wedding in Crossroads and probably the biggest. Two very head- strong people from different backgrounds had found a way to make a relationship work. Jack and Molly Payne lived out the rest of their years on that farm training pointers and guiding hunters from around the area. It was a marriage that most folks thought would never work.

"It worked because the two loved each other. It was a love that was stronger than all their differences," Uncle Lee said as he sat up in bed. "Now Joe, I don't think it will matter that much whether you think Mattie asked you to marry her or you asked Mattie. The real question is, do you really love each other? I have known Mattie all her life. She deserves a man who will treat her like a queen and love her with all his heart. If you can do that, then you have my blessing."

"Uncle Lee, someway I think that story was told in such a way that it was a lesson for me. I know how much Mattie cares about you. You have been like a grandfather to her all of her life. She must have been the granddaughter that you never had. You have also been a very special person to me over the past months. I will always appreciate the way you have invited me into your life. If Mattie and I get married and ever have a son it will be an honor for us to name him Lee," Joe replied.

CHAPTER SIXTEEN

THE DEATH OF A TOWN

By the evening it was clear to Joe and Mattie that Uncle Lee did not have long to live. Joe convinced Mattie that he should spend the night in the room with Uncle Lee. They found a waiting room with a fold-out chair for Mattie so that she could rest.

During the night Uncle Lee began to talk about his childhood. He called several times for his parents and other members of his family. Joe tried to encourage him to sleep, but he was restless and unaware of where he was or what he was saying.

The following morning the doctor on call at the hospital suggested that Uncle

Lee had experienced a stroke in the night. He ordered some medicine that he thought would help him rest. He told Joe that they should be prepared for another stroke at any time. It was his opinion that he would not live through the day.

At eleven o'clock on Christmas Eve Uncle Lee passed away in his sleep. It was a difficult time for both Joe and Mattie. Mattie had planned the funeral service as Uncle Lee had requested, but carrying out those plans was more difficult than she had expected.

When a person lives to be ninety-six years of age, they out live all of the people of their generation. Uncle Lee had even out lived his family members. Mattie knew that the service would only be attended by a few people who really knew Uncle Lee. She could not keep from thinking about how unfair that seemed. But as Uncle Lee had told her in planning his funeral that was just the way life was.

There was snow on the ground at the cemetery, and it was cold for a grave-side service. But that was what Uncle Lee had requested. Four young men from the local church provided the music, and the pastor read some scripture. It was clear to Joe and Mattie that they did their jobs without much compassion. Probably because they had never met Uncle Lee.

Mattie's mind went back to all the times Uncle Lee had played the fiddle and organ for her. He played with such emotion that it gave the songs so much meaning. How she wished that these young men could have just heard him play and sing. Oh, how much they could have learned about music from him.

Then Mattie's attention shifted to the pastor's message. Uncle Lee had lived in the community all of his life. He had been active in the church, school, and community for years. This pastor had worked with the church not more than two miles from Uncle Lee's house for ten years and he had never visited him. The words of encouragement sounded as though he knew nothing about Uncle Lee or his life.

Some of the things that Uncle Lee had shared with Mattie about life began to race through her mind. He had sat in his rocking chair beside the road and watched people rushing here and there. All were too busy to give enough time from their busy schedules to stop and learn a real lesson about life from a man of great wisdom.

How fortunate she had been to know this man she called Uncle Lee.

The defensive wall that Mattie had built around her life for protection against all the cruel things that people said about her and her father was breaking down, and she could not stop it. Her mind began to recall some of the things she had heard her father say in his sermons. She was only a child at the time he preached, but the words came flying back as if they had been said last week.

Mattie's father had been so influenced by Fancy Burger that he had something to say about Isaiah's experience in every sermon. According to her father, God was always seeking those who would listen and answer His call. She sure wasn't interested in His call, not now. She did her best to forget that time in her life. She didn't want anything to do with Fancy Burger's message or God's call.

Mattie was glad when the pastor prayed his last prayer and came by to shake hands with her. She could go home and busy herself with farm work. There was plenty to do. After all, Uncle Lee had told her that when the time came for him to die, she was to move on with her life. That was what he wanted, and that was what she was going to do.

The few people who attended the funeral passed by to express their concern for Mattie and share a word or two. Because of the snow and cold day everyone left the cemetery rather quickly. Mattie was sure it wasn't because she was a Haines, Gene Haines' daughter.

Joe drove Mattie back to her farm. He offered to stay and help her do the work that needed to be done, but Mattie wanted to be alone. Mattie quickly began the feeding of the animals for the cold night that was coming. Try as she did she could not get Fancy Burger off her mind.

"I didn't even know the man," she said to herself. "I have just lost the last person who really cared about me, and I am thinking about a man I never knew. God calling, what in the world would God want of me. I am a Haines, surely He knows that. They say He is suppose to know everything."

Mattie finished the chores and returned to the house to prepare a meal. She wasn't hungry, but she had to eat something. The church had not offered to prepare a meal for the people, and Mattie had not eaten since breakfast. As she entered the house, she could hear the telephone ringing. It wasn't the right time for her to talk to anyone on the phone, so she decided to let it ring. Before she could change clothes and make her way to the kitchen, the phone was ringing again.

"Hello," Mattie answered.

"I don't think it is a good idea for you to be alone tonight. I will come over and stay with you if you will permit me to," Joe said.

"Now wouldn't that be all I need to put a black mark on a perfect reputation. Can't you just hear the folks all over the area talking about that. Joe Harrison took advantage of a weeping young Mattie Haines and moved in to spend the night with her," Mattie answered shedding tears as she spoke.

"I don't care what people are going to say. You need someone, and I am just the person you need. I will be there in less than one hour," Joe responded.

"I guess you will expect a full meal on the table when you arrive. Well, I don't feel like cooking tonight, Joe Harrison. You just go over to Sid's and enjoy his banana pie," Mattie said as she slammed the phone down.

"Now why did I say that," she said to herself. "The only man I have ever considered marrying, and I treat him like that."

In less than one hour Joe knocked on Mattie's door. He had a banana pie from Sid's with all the food needed for a good meal.

"I know you are in a bad mood, and I don't have any problem with that. I would be too. But you have got to eat, and I don't care what people will say," Joe said as he placed the food on the table. "After we eat, we have some serious talking to do. You have put me off long enough. It is time you give me an answer."

"I guess you mean an answer to whether I am willing to marry you or not. Well, I don't see this as the right time to deal with a question like that," Mattie said as she helped Joe with the food.

"Your life has just changed. It will never be the same again. I understand that. I went through something similar to this with the loss of my wife and children. But we can have each other, and we can build a good life together. And I don't need to hear about what other folks think. It is our future; we can't change the past, but we sure can make a beautiful future," Joe explained.

"Well, Mr. Know-It-All, I didn't know that people could predict the future. Tell me, what do you see in 'our' future?" Mattie asked.

"I see two people doing anything they want to do. We can stay here, or we can move anywhere we want to go," Joe said.

"And how are we going to make a living. Are you planning on herding chickens, or maybe building houses? I have seen you make an effort at those jobs, and I haven't been impressed. And what about my farm?" Mattie asked.

"It is difficult to let go of something, or place you have had for some time, but it can be done. I did it, and I can do it again. With you beside me, it will be easier this time," Joe explained.

"Joe, have you given any more thought to what the Bible says in Isaiah about God calling people?" Mattie asked as she sat down at the table and looked at Joe with a look he had never seen on her face before.

"Oh, Mattie, I don't think this is the time to bring up something like that," he said searching for the right words to use for an answer.

"It's the right time to talk about marriage, selling my farm and your house, moving anywhere we want to move, but it isn't the right time to talk about the Bible?

I guess you have lost me. If I remember correctly, it was you who brought this matter up some time ago. You thought it was the right time when you brought it up," Mattie replied.

"Okay, I am willing to listen. What do you want to say about this Isaiah thing? Are you going to suggest that you feel like Isaiah, and you think you hear God calling?" Joe asked in a tone that expressed his displeasure in the subject.

"I may feel a little like Isaiah. I think he had just lost his leader, and his world had fallen apart. Uncle Lee held my world together. Anytime I had a problem, he was the only person I had that I could trust for a good answer. Yes, I think I feel a little like Isaiah," Mattie answered.

"And do you hear God calling? If you do, what is He saying? Is He asking you to go somewhere for Him?" Joe asked in a way that seemed to be poking fun at Mattie.

"I should have known. No matter how you dress men, they are all the same. I think I see your thinking now. We were going to create a beautiful life together as long as we did what you wanted to do," Mattie said as she picked up the banana pie from the table and threw it at Joe. "Now I think I have had enough of you, so get out of 'MY' house!" Mattie screamed.

"I'm not leaving." Joe replied. "I have made a fool out of myself, and I intend to stay here until you help me clean up this banana pie. Then I want you to tell me what you want to do in the future," Joe said as he began to clean up the pie.

Joe and Mattie spent the night talking about their future. Mattie agreed that she loved Joe enough to marry him, and she was willing to do that, after they worked out a plan for the future. Joe listened as Mattie shared her ideas of things they could do with their lives. After all their ideas were exhausted, Mattie raised the question of what God might want them to do.

Two weeks after the death of Uncle Lee, Joe and Mattie got married. They sold their homes in Elbow and Turnbow and moved to Texas. Joe entered a Bible school to study for the mission field, and Mattie entered a singing school to develop her talent in music so that she could help Joe. God had called and they had answered.

It is difficult to suggest that one specific event caused the death of a town. Uncle Lee believed that the boys' basketball team winning the state championship was the main factor in the death of Crossroads (Elbow). He also saw Sadie's run-in with Dr. Rogers and Pete Albright's wagon as part of the cause. But overall, losing the school was something that the town just could not overcome.

History has shown that consolidation of schools did take the heart out of many small communities in the Ozarks. Railroads also created towns and then contributed to their deaths when they ceased to run trains through the area. Highways later took the place of railroads in contributing to the growth or decline of towns in the Ozarks. Most people would say that many factors contributed to the deaths of towns like Elbow.

One thing seems clear about the death of this town. When Uncle Lee died, the history of the town as only he could tell it died. The highway bypassed the town and the door was closed on the community forever.

When you drive down highway nine and you come to the new gas station and all the buildings that exist to take your money, you might want to stop. Look across the road in the big field to the south of the gas station. The signs on the fence say 'keep out,' so you will have to look as hard as possible with your imagination.

All the buildings are gone. The streets have grown up with grass and brush. The cemetery has grown over with trees. Someone has taken Fancy Burger's tombstone. But really use your imagination, don't you see it? There is Stella's boarding house, the trophy case, the gym that had so many exciting ball games. Can't you just hear Fancy preaching at the top of his voice to a church filled with people?

Now look east up the road to the big Oak trees. Can't you see the old house and the rocking chair there beside the road?

Oh, Joe and Mattie wanted me to ask you, Is God calling?

DE3 27G

mD8 J9W

Made in the USA
Charleston, SC
06 June 2014